TENDERBEAR GOES APESHIT

BIX SKAHILL

Thicke & Vaney Books
Purveyors of Fair to Middling Works

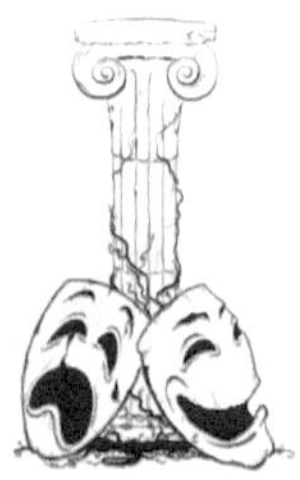

*To my father, who would have hated it
and Bradley Sands, who did.*

GUNILLINGUS

Sure as shit, if Deputy Sheriff Krispy Krowbart ever got Reba McEntire into the boudoir, he'd open up a big old bag of nasty. Give the Queen of Country Music the time of her life. If she lived.

One thing he wanted to do to the rodent-faced chanteuse was a little bit of magic he called gunillingus. That's where one takes their trusty sidearm, preferably a .44 that's killed a body, just like the one strapped to his hip, and work said weaponry into a lady's love swamp. In and out, in and out. Till it gets nice and juicy. Then remove said weapon and shove it deep into your lady friend's pie hole. Make her lick herself off the barrel.

Gunillingus. Only in America. You gotta love it.

Not that Deputy Sheriff Krispy Krowbart had ever performed such a perverted act. That would have taken a willing accomplice and he'd only had sex with one female in his life, Mrs. Deputy Sheriff Krispy Krowbart. She was a bit of a stick in the mud, sex-wise. Missionary, Saturday night, lights off. No butt stuff. Preferably no orgasms.

Another roadblock to his gunillingus-with-Reba-McEntire scenario was that he didn't know the country singer personally. Never been to a concert. Didn't own any of her music. But he had her picture taped up in his locker down at the Fauquier County Sheriff's Office. To him, she looked like a minx even if he wasn't quite sure what a minx was. He supposed it was some kind of rodent who loved doing the nasty.

Though he didn't know the sultry rodent of a country star, there wasn't a day that passed that he didn't fantasize about pouring the steaming cobs to her.

It wasn't against the law for a guy to dream. That's what the Good Lord put us on earth for. To dream, to hope, to pray, to die.

The sheriff was presently doing his hoping parked in his patrol car at the edge of a gravel road near Sumerduck, Virginia. His dick in his hand and Reba McEntire, naked and squirming, in the boudoir of his mind.

It was 3 AM. Nothing around but crickets and stars. Acres and acres of secluded silence.

Although he was technically on the clock, Deputy Sheriff Krispy Krowbart was about as far from patrolling for lawless scum as he could get. Off the beaten track so he could please his pisser in peace.

Just the way the Good Lord wanted us to do hand-to-gland combat.

Some might interpret this as negligence of duty, but the deputy sheriff knew there was no duty to be done. Fauquier County was peaceful, for the most part. Sure there were times when some of the high school boys got a little groat in their gander and acted up, tipping cows or scaring the blacks or whatnot, but for the most part, Krowbart whiled away his hours tossing the ham javelin.

Things were going along quite nicely in the polishing of the lighthouse department when he heard a sound. An engine, far off, but growing closer. Growling. Driving fast, driving mean.

Christ on a bike, he thought, *could a man not bop one's baloney without the intrusions of modern day living?*

With a heavy sigh, he returned his dick to its polyester tomb and waited.

He was going to bust this lawless mothertrucker, bust him good. Reckless driving, hopefully find some drugs, maybe a few illegal weapons.

Reba gone, Krowbart now dreamed of the perp resisting arrest. This was his favorite pastime. Some meth head trying to prove his metal. Gave the deputy sheriff an excuse to work out some of his frustrations.

The roar of the car grew. Obviously muffler-less. Some hick coming home from a good time.

Deputy Sheriff Krispy Krowbart added disturbing the peace to his list and grinned.

Over the hill behind him charged a dented Chevy. Puke green, cracked windshield, dents running the length of its body. Weaving down the gravel road, kicking up dust. The windows down, the system up. Cranking *Sweet Home Alabama* full volume.

This gave Krowbart pause. His love of rebel songs clouded, for a moment, his judgement. As an officer of the law he couldn't publicly display his fondness for the Confederacy. But at home he was a free man of his own making. He had Stars and Bars coffee mugs, flower vases, and toilet seats. Even the towel he masturbated into every night, save Saturday night, was a terrycloth copy of the glorious Confederate battle flag.

But if he thought the music gave him pause, when he spied who, or rather what, was driving the wrecked automobile, every fibre in his body stopped and stared.

Behind the wheel of the Chevy was a bear, pink and fluffy, with large plastic eyes and a perma-grin. Atop his head: a sailor cap cocked at a jaunty angle. Using only one paw to command the vehicle, he chugged from a 40 of Mickey's with the other. Laughing, the bear took a long, spilly swill.

In the not too distant past, bears had been a rare occurrence in Fauquier County, but of late, folks had started spying black bears in their backyards.

Of course, no one had ever seen a bear this faggy around these parts. That's not to say that the deputy sheriff didn't recognize the bear. Or, at least, thought he recognized the bear.

"No, no, no," he said to the crickets, the stars. "This just can't be."

The Chevy blew past him, kicking up a cloud of dust, not bothering to slow down or swerve. Missed the patrol car by a gnat's ass.

It took the shaken lawman a moment to act. Switching on the lights, the siren, peeling out. Kicking rocks.

When he heard the siren, the bear tossed the beer bottle into the night. An arc of pissy malt liquor and green glass. But he didn't pull over. Didn't even slow down.

Krowbart felt his patrol car swerve and swish on the gravel. He had a hard time holding it on the road. In a safety meeting not long ago in Warrenton, some hotshot from the Justice Department had come in and tried to teach them a thing or two about car chases. This liberal mouthpiece said sometimes it was best to let the perpetrator go, if you were endangering yourself or others.

Funk that, thought Krowbart. He had to catch this joker, had to find out if his eyes were funning him.

The chase went on for a few miles, over hill and dale, the cop not gaining an inch on the wrecked Chevy. When they careened around Bluegrass Road Corner, the bear didn't career so hot and his vehicle shot off the road. Took flight. Crashed into the lavender field beyond. Flipping a few times, it came to a rest on its roof. Busted beyond recognition, steam rising.

Krowbart skidded to a stop, keeping the crashed vehicle in his headlights. Jumping from the patrol car, he pulled his .44, which always made his hands feel itchy.

Gun aimed, he made his way through the ditch, through the lavender. All the wheels on the Chevy were still spinning but there was no movement from inside the vehicle.

The deputy sheriff feared the occupant dead, which made his heart sink, as he would not get an opportunity to interrogate the sumabitch. And there'd be paperwork. Deputy Sheriff Krispy Krowbart abhorred paperwork. It was like being in school again and learning had never been his thing.

When he was ten feet shy of the Chevy, Krowbart detected movement in the shadows. He stopped, took up a shooting stance, waited.

Ever so slowly, ginger as a cat in a rocking chair factory, the bear crawled out of the smashed window of the car. Stood. Dusted himself off. Regarded the cop.

A flashy pink bear in a field of exploding purple flowers. Would have really been a sight to see if Krowbart wasn't so traumatized.

It was just as he feared.

He'd seen some weird doings in his time behind the badge – most of it pertaining to lonely farmers taking to their animal husbandry with a little too much vigor – but this crapola took the cake and ate it too.

Shaking his head, which didn't do no good, he said, "Tenderbear... is that you?"

Tenderbear belched. Adjusted the hat on his head, the only clothing he wore. "L'Chaim."

"Excuse me?"

"*L'Chaim*, motherfucker, *l'chaim.*"

The sheriff put on his frowniest frown. The one he used on longhairs, midgets, and women. "What kind of Commie crap you spewing there, Tenderbear?"

The spokesanimal didn't respond. Not with words at least. He growled and charged, head down.

Though the plushy beast was ostensibly running, he wasn't getting anywhere real fast.

Krowbart was trapped between a rock and another rock. On one hand, he loved shooting living things. On the other, Tenderbear was a beloved spokesanimal. Krispy Krowbart and the missus were just two of his millions of fans across this great county. Any time one of his commercials came on, not only did the Krowbarts not mute it, they turned it up. Considered it high entertainment.

On the other other hand, Krowbart would be damned if he was gonna get mauled to death by a fictitious bear who couldn't drive worth a damn.

Raising his gun, the sheriff mentally prepared himself to snuff out another of the Lord's creatures.

Fate, as it is want to do, intervened.

Just a few feet shy of Krowbart, Tenderbear stopped, collapsed to his pink knees, and vomited sausagey chunks all over the cop's shoes.

Rolling over on his back, Tenderbear looked up at the stars and shouted, "Now my bottom feels like it's back on top!"

THE QUICKEST WAY TO
A MAN'S HEART

From Giles Moribund's 108th floor penthouse, he had a perfect view of Lady Liberty's ass.

"Really makes you believe in America," he told anyone who would listen, and even more who wouldn't.

Everything about Giles' penthouse was super classy. All the furniture was either gold or onyx or gold-plated onyx. His silverware was carved from whalebone, his art expensive and obtuse and mostly nudes, his pillows filled with dodo feathers. The television was encased in a bigger television, which was, in turn, encased in massive television.

In his bedroom was a four-poster bed once owned by Thomas Jefferson. Whenever he assfucked one of his cavalcade of whores, he liked to pretend they were Sally Hemings - though white, of course - and, while he thrust with gusto, enjoyed quoting from the Declaration of Independence at length.

It was his third favorite piece of literature after the Bible and "THIS NOTE IS LEGAL TENDER FOR ALL DEBTS, PUBLIC AND PRIVATE."

Currently in the majestic four-poster, there were no declarations happening nor any going up the old dirt road. Just Giles sleeping unsoundly, as he always did. Tossing, turning, nightmares of failure.

On the onyx nightstand Giles' gold-plated phone rang.

Swearing, the very, very, very rich man sat up and answered. "Moribund here... What the hell... Tenderbear... arrested... Virginia... a *brith milah*?"

He slammed the phone down hoping something would shatter. Nothing did. Onyx and gold are like that.

Running a shaking hand through his thinning blonde hair, the owner of Moribund Advertising lay back down and studied himself in the mirror which hung above his bed. Despite all his surgeries and pills and creams, Giles was beginning to look his age. He frowned at his frown lines.

The shape beside him, sleeping beneath black sheets fashioned from Algerian spider webs, stirred. Like a migratory bird, the whore's hand found his flaccid cock, squeezed.

Needing all his blood to bemoan his fate, Giles swatted her advances away and climbed from the bed. He studied himself in the mirror that hung beside the mirror that hung above his bed. His skin was too gray, his tummy too flabby, his penis still not impressive enough. He would have to call Dr. Feldspar, Dr. Cranberry, and Drs. Hopesprings and Eternal.

But first, first he had to figure out what he was going to do about the Tenderbear debacle.

Pacing the onyx floor in slippers fabricated from the souls of dolphins, Giles vowed to kill Allan Krapowitz with his bare hands.

"Come back to bed," said the whore, still hidden beneath the sheets of spider webs.

"What you don't seem to understand, you filthy harlot, is that I have an international incident on my hands here!"

But the whore didn't care about his business woes. She cast off the sheets and thrust her alabaster ass high into the air. Her brown eye winked at him. That stopped Giles in his tracks; the whore knew the quickest way to a man's heart.

Forgetting all about Tenderbear and Sumerduck, Virginia and *brith milahs*, Giles jumped onto the bed. Not bad for an eighty year old man. With nary a nod toward foreplay, he entered the whore, and roared toward the mirrored heavens. Taking all his aggression out on her ass.

"They are endowed by their Creator with certain unalienable rights!"

Thrust, thrust, thrust.

The whore squealed, "Now my bottom feels like it's back on top!"

Everyone was familiar with Tenderbear's catchphrase.

MACRAMANIA

Waitressing at the Gastrofocker Café in Normal, Iowa for over twenty years had turned Flo Mylarson into something of a psychologist. She could read people, their moods, what kind of pie they needed.

When Moses Guttchenridder wandered in that morning, Flo frowned. She'd always liked Moses, found him dashing with his long blonde hair, clear blue eyes, and ever-present stoner smile. But he wasn't smiling now, which wasn't new. For the last few weeks he hadn't been acting like himself. He was sullen, exhausted, short tempered.

She approached him with a smile, trying to lighten his mood. "Morning, Moses. Looks like you could use some peach cobbler."

"Just coffee, Flo," he said, rubbing his eyes, yawning.

She patted his arm. "You'll feel better when your mom gets back into town. When does she come back again?"

"In a few days. I hope."

"It seems odd she would just pack up and--"

"The coffee, Flo, please."

"Oh, yeah, sure. You gotta get Macramania open."

"No, not today. The shoppe is going to be closed today. Again."

"Because you-."

"Just because. I need some coffee, Flo, and I need it right now!"

Nodding, she padded off, shaking her head under her breath.

AMERICA'S NUMBER TWO
TOILET PAPER

Regan Moribund played with herself listlessly while gazing out her office window at the Manhattan skyline. She was on the phone, talking in a throaty voice that Giles, who was lingering in the doorway, had never heard.

She arched her back, flicked her red hair. Her neck so thin, so white.

"Of course I'm touching myself. Yes, yes, yes you're the randy janitor and I'm the naughty Catholic school girl with a secret."

Slightly turned on, but unable to bear it any longer, Giles cleared his throat.

Jerking her hand away from her undercarriage, Regan spun. Informing the person on the other end of the line that something had come up, she slammed the phone down. It shattered.

Entering his daughter's office, Giles snapped, "I hope those words of love were for your cock-eyed husband."

"Father, I've been divorced from Charlie for over a year, as you know, and he didn't have a cock-eye, he suffered from astigmatism," said Regan, straightening her dress.

"Well, pardon me for not being able to keep your lustlife straight but it's like Grand Central Station down in your bacon hole."

Sighing, Regan, "Once again, Father, you are misdirecting your anger at me. What you are really upset about is the Tenderbear arrest."

"Tenderbear wasn't arrested, Regan, Allan Krapowitz was. Tenderbear is a spokesanimal that is loved the world over; Allan Krapowitz is a drunken fuckbrain who is single-handedly trying to destroy me and my company. Which is all your fault, in my opinion. You're in charge of keeping that wily Jew in line, yet you let him travel to Virginia unchaperoned."

"As I've explained many times before, I don't like traveling with Allan. He can't keep his pink paws off my lady bits."

"Ha! You've had so many paws on your lady bits, the FBI could use your mossy donut as their national fingerprint data base."

"But Krapowitz is even too creepy for me. He wanted to play hide the salami while he was wearing his bear suit."

"Well, thanks to your aversion to a little ursine love, our beloved Tenderbear is now rotting in some backwater hoosegow and my career is in the shitter. How do you think the fine people at KrapKo, our biggest client and manufacturers of America's Number Two toilet paper, Krap-Wad, are going to react to all this negative publicity surrounding their spokesanimal?"

Standing, Regan, "I've been telling you for years that we should shitcan Tenderbear. My market research shows millennials don't care for--"

Turning crimson, Giles marched toward his daughter, got right in her face. "No, never! I will not hear such blasphemy. Tenderbear was the first spokesanimal I ever created, back in 1988, which, I might add, was before I created you."

With a hitch in her voice, Regan said, "Yes, and you love that damn bear more than you love me!"

"Regan, I would love to say that's ridiculous, but, right at this moment, I'm afraid I can't."

Eyes burning, they glared at one another for a moment before Giles stomped out. Over his shoulder, "We have an emergency meeting at KrapKo in an hour and you'd better have some fucking ideas or I'll fire you. I'm sorry Regan, I know you're family, but this is a family business."

PERFECT WEREWOLF HAIR

As he waited for his coffee, which he needed to hopefully trigger his poop system, Moses Guttchenridder watched a team of flies tempt fate by darting between the blades of the lazy ceiling fan hanging above the counter of the Gastrofocker Café.

Flo finally waddled up with his cup of joe. She was rotund, had bleach blonde hair, and talked too damn much for Moses' liking.

"You look beat, Moses."

"It was a long night."

"What were you doing?"

He looked at her with drooping eyes but didn't answer. Just took a long slurp of coffee. "I was... I was doing some intense macramé stuff."

"You gotta watch yourself. Hobbies can be serious business. Did I ever tell you about my cousin and her Precious Moments fanaticism."

Flo had told Moses this inane story a hundred times.

He said, "She sold her kids."

"She sold her kids. Just so she could travel down to that Precious Moments Chapel in Carthage, Missouri. And the crazy thing, it was closed for remodeling when she got there."

"That's a heartbreaking story," said Moses, who wasn't really listening.

She nodded, went to fill the sugar bowls.

At the end of the counter sat a TV. Tiny, black and white. The news was on and Moses perked up when a story about the Sigma Omega Sigma Killer came on. The owner of Macramania, like every other American, was following this story closely. A serial killer was traveling the highways and byways of this great country, murdering and decapitating the men who'd resided in the Sigma Omega Sigma house at the University of Illinois in 1992.

According to the ancient TV, the previous evening another fraternity brother had been killed and his head stolen. This one in Enid, Oklahoma.

Suddenly, Flo loomed out of nowhere. Moses nearly spilled his coffee. "Can you believe all them poor fraternity brothers getting killed?"

"Yeah, it's, it's really... it's really bad."

"And why would the killer take their heads?"

Moses could only shrug. He had no idea why.

On the TV, the news anchor, who had perfect werewolf hair, cleared his throat. "And finally, here's an interesting story coming out of Sumerduck, Virginia. Last night, Allan Krapowitz was arrested for driving while under the influence. Who is Allan Krapowitz you might ask? Good question. Well, for the last fifteen years Allan has been wearing the suit of Tenderbear, Krap-Wad toilet paper's beloved spokesanimal."

Over the anchor's shoulder appeared the mug shot of Tenderbear, an archipelago of vomit down his fluffy chin.

SEX WITH EVERY MEMBER
OF MENUDO

Watching a sweaty Giles Moribund storm from Regan's office, Quentin Quartermaster had to hide his smirk. As Regan's assistant, he'd been sitting right outside her door and he'd heard every delectable word. It was like sex with every member of Menudo when Giles ripped Regan a new one, which was happening quite a lot these days.

"Quentin, get in here now! I need a schedule a quick massage with Henric and his wonderful wandering hands!"

Rolling his eyes, plotting his revenge, Quentin pulled up his boss' schedule on his computer.

He could physically feel his facade as the sassy but supportive gay personal assistant starting to crack.

AN ATTEMPT AT DEFECATION

Back at his house, Moses Guttchenridder was sitting on his toilet, waiting for a bowel movement he knew wouldn't come, when Thorax the Thoroughly Miffed burst into the bathroom.

It would be nice, for Moses' mental sanity, to say that he was surprised to see a magical garden gnome come crashing into his existence, all plaster and bluster, but that, sadly, was not the case. Thorax had been ruining his existence for the last month, ever since coming to life.

"Why be ye sitting?" Thorax asked in his thick but unplaceable accent.

"Well, dude, I'm attempting to defecate."

Thorax rushed him and Moses shied away as much as one can whilst sitting on the john. Though the garden gnome was small and dressed in jaunty elfin clothing, he was a mean son-of-a-bitch who didn't hesitate to kill.

But Moses knew that Thorax wouldn't harm him. The deadly magical garden gnome needed him. For now.

"Ye listen to me, son of Moår, there be not time for sitting as we have little of the clock left to rid Arth of those bastards who wronged my people."

"Yeah, I know, I know, you've only told me that like a million times. Jesus, dude, calm down. We just got back from Enid an hour ago, give me a break."

"Okay, son of Moår, I leave ye be. But mind, we have only two moons left to finish our glorious task. I be in yon kitchen, cleaning Awful Tine, the Sword of Might and Forbearance."

On the way out, stomping his tiny feet, the garden gnome slammed the door.

Moses shook his head. Since they'd begun their killing spree, Moses hadn't had a restful moment. Or a good shit.

AT A JAUNTY ANGLE

In the boardroom of KrapKo sat a long mahogany table surrounded by several members of the Krapowitz family. All of them scowling. The objects of their scorn sat at the far end of the table: Giles Moribund and his daughter Regan.

The CEO of KrapKo, Handjob Smokestack Krapowitz III, started the meeting. "Mr. Moribund, I hope you have a way to get us out of this media quagmire."

"Of course. We'll do a national search for a new actor to carry on the Tenderbear mantle--"

"I'm not talking about replacing our worthless drunken cousin, that's a given. The man blew chunks on a state trooper. I'm talking about Tenderbear himself."

"Oh, yes, certainly. I'm working on some big changes for Tenderbear. I was thinking – and tell me if this seems too drastic – of ditching the sailor cap and replacing it with a pith helmet."

A Second Krapowitz said, "Still cocked at a jaunty angle, I hope."

"You know it!"

In a clear voice that rang out like a shot, Regan asked, "Who wipes their ass?"

Jaws dropped, time turned into cement as several Krapowitzs cleared their throats uncomfortably.

Out of the corner of his mouth, Giles warned his daughter to pipe down.

She didn't, she stood. "It's a simple question. Who in this room wipes their ass? I do. After defecating, I wipe my ass. The President of the United States wipes his ass, Bradley Cooper wipes his ass and you all, presumably, wipe your asses or have servants or loved ones who do it for you. You know who doesn't wipe their ass? Bears."

Giles said, "Regan, I demand that you stop this insanity."

"No Giles," said Handjob, "let this semi-hot female speak."

"What I'm suggesting is that KrapKo needs a spokes*person* for Krap-Wad toilet paper."

The Second Krapowitz asked, "Like Bradley Cooper?"

Excited, a Third chimed in, "Or the President?"

A Fourth said, "Oh, I like the smell of that bacon."

Shaking his head, Handjob, "They both seem rather busy."

"No," said Regan, "I'm not talking about an entertainer or a politician or anyone famous. I mean a normal person, the Everyman. The Everyman who wipes his ass with Krap-Wad toilet paper.

The Third Krapowitz asked, "Will he still wear a hat?"

The First, "At a jaunty angle?"

"Certainly, gentlemen, but he'll wear whatever kind of hat a normal person wears."

The fourth said, "Oh, I like the ring of them bells."

Looking around desperately, licking his lips, Giles said, "This... this is preposterous."

Handjob said, "I like it too. So, Giles' female offspring, where does one find one of these normal people?"

"For the last week, gentlemen, I've been studying a map of the United States, looking for a town that smacked of normality and, I believe, I have found such a town. Normal, Iowa."

"Really?" asked Handjob. "There's a town called Normal?"

The Second Krapowitz, "There's really a state called Iowa?"

The First, "That sounds jaunty."

The Fourth, "I like fur on that fox."

Smiling, Regan said, "Then we're all in agreement. Let's find our new spokesperson."

As if performing a magic trick, she pulled a slender White Pages telephone directory from her purse. Flipping it open, she closed her eyes and ran a finger down a random page.

Pleaded Giles, "This... this is ridiculous. We need test groups and market analysis and all that shit."

Handjob waved his hand at Giles to silence him.

Stopping her finger, Regan opened her eyes and reached for the phone at the center of the conference table. "Here you go, gentlemen. The new face of Krap-Wad toilet paper is normal person... Moses Guttchenridder."

TOO LUMPY FOR HUMAN CONSUMPTION

While Thorax the Thoroughly Miffed cleaned the blood from Awful Tine, the Sword of Might and Forbearance, Moses attempted to eat his oatmeal, but found it was too lumpy for human consumption.

That's how Moses' life had been since purchasing the evil garden gnome at a garage sale: hard to swallow. It was a total bummer. He rued that purchase with all his heart. It was even worse than that time he bought that Taylor Swift CD.

The phone next to the refrigerator rang, shattering the morning. Putting down his towel, Thorax said, "That device infernal, who wishes to communicate with you now?"

"How am I supposed to know, dude?" asked Moses, standing. Crossing to the phone, he picked up the receiver despite the fact he didn't recognize the area code on the caller ID. "Listen, if this is some charity or scam or whatever, I'm not interested, and I don't need you to harsh my mellow right at this very moment in time as I am dealing with several issues. Not the least of which is some very uneatable oatmeal."

A woman said in a clipped voice, "Mr. Guttchenridder, what I'm selling is power and glory."

"Oh, religion. No thanks, I've had enough of that for one lifetime."

"No, what I'm talking about is better than religion, it's advertising. Mr. Guttchenridder, can you spare me a minute to change your life?"

Though he didn't really understand what she was saying, this lady had such a nice voice he could have listened to her all day.

He looked over his shoulder. Thorax was glaring at him. Slowly, slowly, slowly polishing the sword that was twice his size "Well, I'm kind of in the middle of something here."

"Mr. Guttchenridder, do you wipe your ass?"

Nearly dropping the phone, he asked, "Whoa, what? This conversation has suddenly turned into a total buzzkill. Who is this?"

"My name is Regan Moribund, I live in New York City and work--"

"Well, Miss Moribund, regardless of how much your voice sounds like a gentle summer breeze, I don't care to be the butt of your joke."

"Please don't be angry, Mr. Guttchenridder, let me explain. I work for KrapKo. Do you use Krap-Wad toilet paper?"

"Well, yeah. I love that Tenderbear."

"Tenderbear is dead. We here at KrapKo are looking for a new face for Krap-Wad toilet paper and we think that face might be you."

This certainly sounded like a prank to Moses, but there was something about this woman's voice that was so real, so genuine, so honest. She reminded him of his dear mother, who was in a state of suspended animation down in the basement.

"Do I have to wear that sailor hat?"

"Not if you don't want to."

Behind him, Moses heard an awful sound. He turned to spy Thorax drawing a whetstone down the long blade of Awful Tine, the Sword of Might and Forbearance, while looking deep into Moses' eyes. Sparks flew.

Returning to the phone, Moses said, "Oh, well, yeah, this is a fairly gnarly offer and all, ma'am, but I'm afraid I'm going to have to say no."

"No?!? But Mr. Guttchenridder, do you understand what I'm offering you? Fame, fortune, and a lifetime's supply of toilet paper."

"That's totally awesome, but I have to go."

He hung up quickly before he could change his mind. Went back to his lumpy oatmeal, avoiding Thorax's eyes.

"Who were ye speaking to on the device so infernal?"

Shrugging, Moses, "Just a telemarketer."

"That is fine, but do not forget the deal we have struck: if any human finds out about our task, ye mother dies."

Moses nodded.

"Good, son of Moår. Tonight we travel to Arlington, Virginia to send Randy Pendleton, purveyor of fine ladies shoes, to the Underworld."

MOSES GUTTCHENRIDDER IS THE ONE

Regan stared at the phone in the center of the conference table. Nothing but dial tone. Even though she'd just been publicly humiliated, she was smiling.

… your voice sounds like a gentle summer breeze…

As if everyone hadn't noticed, Giles said, "Well, it appears the young man hung up on us."

Though she wouldn't look at him, Regan felt her father's smirk burning.

The Second Krapowitz said, "That man doesn't sound very normal to me."

The Fourth, "Yeah, I don't like the nuts on that busboy."

"Perhaps," suggested Handjob, "we should try someone else in Normal, Iowa."

"Oh," said the Fourth, "I like the cock hanging off that cliff diver."

Staring into the distance, Regan said, "No, Moses Guttchenridder is the one. Now I am sure of that. I will fly out there tomorrow morning to make this happen."

A BRIEF BURST OF HISTORY

Jehwawa Krapowitz was born in Krakow in 1891. At the age of four, he dropped out of school to work at his father's wildly unpopular store: Rinds-R-Us. At 19, looking for a better, less rind-filled future, Krapowitz packed his bags and set sail for America. Aboard his ship, he encountered a beautiful young woman, Ellen Wadstein, a fellow passenger in sub-steerage. They met when she approached him and offered to have sexual relations with him for a dollar. Though he considered this a fair price, Krapowitz had to decline due to the fact that he'd forgotten to bring his wallet with him.

"You pinhead," said Ellen kindly, "how do you expect to get by in America without a shekel to your name?"

He shrugged and asked if she had any money. Cackling in her native tongue, she showed him her purse, which was bursting with dollar bills.

Shocked, he asked, "Where did you get all that money?"

Now it was her turn to shrug. She offered to buy him a cup of coffee. At the Sub-Steerage Café, she spent an inordinate amount of time licking her lips and she knew a great number of the other male passengers by name.

"How do you know so many people?" asked Krapowitz.

Again, a shrug. "So turdbrain, what's your broke ass going to do in America?"

His face lit up, for Krapowitz had a dream. He was going to build a toilet paper empire, starting small, by selling single sheets door-to-door.

This young man spoke with such enthusiasm that Ellen could not help but fall in love with him, despite the fact that he was borderline imbecilic.

That night, she pulled him behind a nearby smokestack and gave him a handjob. She was kind enough to charge him half-price – what she referred to as the "boyfriend special"– and allow him to start a tab.

Being a virgin, Krapowitz was so excited that someone else was touching his schlong, he kept shouting the names of his favorite pastries throughout the act.

Just as he reached orgasm, the ship struck an iceberg.

He said, "Boy, they weren't kidding when they said that sex felt like the earth moving."

"We've struck something, you dolt!"

Holding hands — though Ellen's was slathered in shimmering dicksplash — the couple joined the long line for the Titanic's lifeboats.

A purser with a walrus mustache kept shouting a bunch of crap about women and children first. Krapowitz had not come this far to have his toilet paper empire dreams flushed down the toilet.

Telling Ellen that he had a plan, he pulled her back into the shadows.

"Listen, Jehwawa, I like you and all, but I don't think this is the time for another handjob. Besides, I'd have to charge you full price this time."

"Hey, is that a polar bear over there?" he shouted, pointing.

When she turned, he struck her in the back of the head. Knocked unconscious, she fell to the deck. He stole her stole and her bursting purse and, promising to never forget her kindness, stepped over her.

Pretending to be a woman by draping the stole over his head and bitching about "how men can't even drive a boat," he took a place in the last lifeboat to be lowered.

Keeping his promise, he never did forget Ellen Wadstein. In fact, he named his toilet paper after both of them: Krap-Wad. And he christened his first-born Handjob Smokestack Krapowitz in her memory.

HE COULD SEE THEIR SKULLS

Wiping away his tears with a Sigma Omega Sigma commemorative beach towel, Randy Pendleton, purveyor of fine ladies shoes, looked out his bedroom window and counted four cops on his lawn. It was the third time he'd counted them in as many minutes. Four cops, all armed, all alert, all waiting for the Sigma Omega Sigma Killer to rear his ugly head.

Their presence did nothing to calm Randy's nerves.

Pendleton returned to shedding tears of fear, pacing the floor. Worrying about whether he would live to see another sunrise.

Glancing up, he noticed the large framed photo that hung above his bed. It was the entire Sigma Omega Sigma crew, gathered on the listing porch of their fraternity house in Champaign, Illinois in 1992. Better times, better times. They were all drunk, all smiling for they'd all just got done having sex with the same woman. Now a great majority – 96% – of those fresh, just-fucked faces were dead, except for two: Pendleton and Crappy.

Pendleton stared at the dead and they stared back. Behind their smiles, he could see their skulls.

Tossing aside the commemorative beach towel in disgust, he ripped the framed photo from the wall and hurled it with all his might. It shattered against the bureau. Glass everywhere.

Huffing, Pendleton felt his stomach rumble like a coal mine explosion. Clutching his abdomen, he skittered toward his bathroom, yet again.

He was beginning to learn that the term "scared shitless" had its roots in reality.

Thank God he'd listened to Tenderbear and really stocked up on toilet paper.

BELOVED TIMESHARE IN PASSAIC

Watching her father pace the elevator, on the verge of a heart attack, Regan couldn't keep the smile off her face.

Giles asked, "What if he's a goat fucker?"

"Excuse me?"

"This is Iowa after all, what if it turns out your man Moses pours the steaming cobs to farm animals or little boys or honey wheat bagels?"

Regan snorted. "He's not that kind of man."

"Oh really? What kind of man is he?"

"The kind kind."

Now it was Giles' turn to snort. "You can tell that by a short phone conversation which ended when he hung up on you?"

"Yes I can."

"You're loony. When we get back to Moribund headquarters, I'll expect your resignation."

"Oh, that won't be happening. For years I've been biding my time, watching you destroy this company, our family name. Now it's my time to shine."

"Sweet Baby G, you really have lost it. If you won't resign, I'll just have to fire you and I'm sure the board will stand by that decision, especially after they hear about the shenanigans that you pulled this morning."

"They already know, Father. In fact, it was their idea that I step in and save Moribund Advertising.

So, ironically, you're the one who's going to resign."

He stopped pacing. He stopped breathing. His skin turned an ashen color one associates with ash. He looked like a statue commemorating failure.

Giles stammered, "But... but..."

"And keep in mind that penthouse where you butt-screw your whores and your fancy fleet of jet skis and your beloved timeshare in Passaic, they all technically belong to the company. So, I'll be expecting a shitload of keys to be landing on my desk after you pack up your office. I know you're family, Father, but this is a family business."

The elevator doors slid open and, with eyes brimming with hatred, Giles Moribund stood shaking and watched his daughter walk away from him.

AKA TENDERBEAR

With his angina acting up, Judge Ponyslapp was hoping for a trouble-free day in his courtroom. When he stepped out of his chambers and saw a man dressed as a giant pink bear standing at the defense table, he felt his dreams go up in smoke.

The asshole hadn't even bothered to clean the vomit from his chin or doff his sailor cap in court.

Droned the court reporter, "The first case on the docket this morning is the *People Vs. Allan Krapowitz.* Mr. Krapowitz has been charged with operating a motor vehicle while under the influence, reckless driving, and vomiting upon a state employee."

Sighing inwardly, Judge Ponyslapp asked the Public Defender, "Mr. Jokes, do you represent this... man?"

"I'm afraid so, sir."

"You might want to inform him it would please the court immensely if he would remove that ridiculous costume."

"I have, your honor. Many times. But Mr. Krapowitz refuses. Or, to be more specific, he growls at me, quite menacingly. Apparently, Mr. Krapowitz is a method actor."

Squinting at the defendant, the Judge asked, "Do I... do I recognize this particular pink bear?"

"You may, sir. He's Tenderbear, the spokesanimal, I

should say *former* spokesanimal, for Krap-Wad toilet paper."

"Former?"

"He was fired this morning via singing telegram."

"It's a cruel world. Please inform Mr. Krapowitz that--"

The pink bear shook his head violently.

"Mr. Jokes, is something wrong with your hirsute client?"

"Well, Judge, I believe he wishes to be referred to solely as 'Tenderbear'."

Under his robes, Judge Ponyslapp rubbed his chest. "Alright. Court reporter please list the defendant as 'Allan Krapowitz, AKA Tenderbear'."

Mr. Jokes said, "Thank you, Your Honor."

Turning back to the defendant's table, Judge Ponyslapp said, "But let your client know his celebrity status, even if his star no longer shines so brightly, will cut no ice in my courtroom."

Tenderbear growled at the bench.

"Mr. Jokes, did your client just growl at me?"

"He did, Your Honor. Although he may have simply been acknowledging you, it's hard to tell. He growls in all sorts of situations."

"Well, in my courtroom, let's endeavor to keep the growling to a minimum, shall we? It's creepy."

"Agreed, sir," said the lawyer.

After scanning a sheaf of papers before him, Ponyslapp said, "So, Mr... ah, Tenderbear here was arrested out on Bluegrass Road, his vehicle weaving from side to side. Drove into the ditch. When the arresting officer pulled him from the wreckage. Mr. Tenderbear proceeded to vomit on him. Are these facts correct as I have stated them?"

"Yes, sir. But I would like the court to know that my client is very sorry for any inconvenience his driving or vomiting may have caused. He was returning from celebrating his nephew's *brith milah* where he might have consumed a little too much Mogen David."

"And what is a *brith milah*, Mr. Jokes? A bear thing?"

"No, sir, it's a Jewish thing."

"Oh, I had no idea Tenderbear was a member of the tribe."

Growling, Tenderbear got to his feet and, with one sweep of his massive pink arm, broke the defendant table in two.

The entire courtroom went apeshit. People screamed in fear, ran away, peed their pants a little in fear.

The Bailiff, who cared for neither bears nor Jews, hustled forward and pinned Tenderbear's arms behind his back while Judge Ponyslapp pounded his gavel, shouting over the pandemonium. "I've had about enough of your animalistic behavior, Mr. Krapowitz, and I order you to serve thirty days in the county jail!"

THE GALLOWS HAND-IN-HAND

Exhausted but smiling, Regan entered her penthouse apartment, having walked all the way from Moribund Advertising, through a gentle summer breeze.

Her pleasant mood was erased by the old man sitting perfectly still on her couch, naked and erect.

Regan started but stifled her scream.

"Where have you been?" Handjob Krapowitz III asked, smiling thinly. "I've been waiting for hours and this couch is really starting to chafe in some very interesting areas."

"I was working late, trying to get things back in order. You might recall, I dethroned my father this morning and he did not go gently into that good night of retirement."

"Oh, you poor thing. I bet you could really go for a bellyful of jizz about right now." Handjob stoked his erection.

Fucking Viagra.

"How'd you get in here? Bribe the doorman with a year's supply of asswipe paper?"

Though the erection remained, the thin smile vanished. "Please, dearest, do not make light of a product that's kept America's behinds clean for a century. And, as for how I gained access to your abode, you gave me a key, remember? Last week, after a rather vigorous bout of the old bone dance where I was pretending to be the wounded WWI flying ace and you were the nasty nurse with the filthy secret."

"Oh, yes." *How could she forget?* Her ass still hurt when it rained.

During this entire interaction, Regan had not moved a muscle. Remained in the foyer. Near the door. Appearing as if she might dash. Handjob rose and, his erection bobbing, crossed to her.

Never before had she noticed how sunken his chest was, how bony his legs, how tiny his penis. He looked ridiculous; he looked like an old man.

Of course, she reminded herself, *I'm not in this relationship for Handjob's rocking body.*

When he hugged her, she had to use every muscle in her body to keep from cringing. He said, "Seeing you grab power in that boardroom today made me so horny."

His tongue lashing out, he tried to kiss her. She turned her head, said, "I wonder what doesn't make you horny, Handjob?"

Reeling in his tongue, he thought about that one for a moment. "Asiago cheese. Asiago cheese doesn't do a damn thing for me, penis-wise. Speaking of my lobknobbber, I want to thrust it into your love furrow."

"Actually, Handjob, dearest, I was thinking of hitting the sack."

He snuggled into her. "As was I, my love, as was I. Now, let's get down to some serious role-playing."

She could feel his tiny erection burrowing into her thigh. Moist breath on her neck. Breaking his hold, she walked toward the balcony, looked out the window at the millions of sparkling lights above and below her.

"You're acting like a woman. What's wrong with you?" he asked.

She shrugged. "I don't know. Maybe I'm just tired."

"Okay, you don't want to do a lot of work, I get it. We'll resort to an old classic. I'll be the wounded knight, felled by the evil dragon, and you can be Maid Marian with a nasty secret."

Grabbing her, he pulled her close. Kissing her neck.

Gently patting his face, she pushed him away. "Handjob, wait. What if we did something a little different tonight?"

"Oh, I like where this is going. You want me to be the randy court jester who was pushed down the castle steps after a particularly humorous imitation of the King and you're the lusty Queen with a nasty secret—."

"No, no. Maybe we could go out for a late dinner or a cup of coffee or just sit around, share a bottle of wine, and talk like normal people."

Glaring at her as if she were talking about socialized medicine, Handjob curled his lip. "But we're not normal people."

"Well, no, but I'm not a queen either. I'm just a tired ad exec who's got a lot on her mind."

"Oh, I see. You want to talk business. Alright, I have an important question for you, how can you be sure this Guttchenridder fellow is the one?"

... your voice sounds like a gentle summer breeze...

"Are you doubting me?" She stiffened in a very negative way.

"What I don't doubt is there are hundreds of ad

agencies in New York City who'd love to get their grubby hands all over the account of America's Number Two toilet paper."

She took a step back, felt as if she were falling. "After everything, after all this..." She waved a hand toward his diminutive dick. "You'd do that to me?"

"Well, I wouldn't even consider it if you simply don the costume I brought for you and started spanking this naughty jester."

Holding back her tears, Regan allowed Handjob to pull her toward the bedroom, though she felt as if they were heading off to the gallows hand-in-hand.

SWEET JESUS' BALLS

There were cops crawling all over the place. Two cruisers sat in the driveway idling, a handful of officers on the lawn. They looked hungry for blood, they looked mean. They looked like cops.

At the dark end of the street sat Moses Guttchenridder in his dented Datsun. Thorax the Thoroughly Miffed sat in the backseat with Awful Tine, the Sword of Might and Forbearance across his lap like a sleeping steel child.

Shaking his head, Moses said, "I don't like the look of this."

Scoffed Thorax, "Just a few weak sentries to get passed."

"They're cops. They have guns and bad tempers. Let's just drive back to Normal and get Randy Pendleton another time."

"Fully aware, are you, Son of Moår, that when the moon's belly grows full, I must return to my slumber. The time is not long for the revenge I seek for my departed brethren. We have only a few more nights to rid Arth of all the brothers of Sigma Omega Sigma."

"Dude, you've killed sixty-three out of sixty-five of these fraternity fucks, don't you think you've kind of made your point?"

"There will be no rest until all of them are dancing

in the flames of the Underworld. Now all you have to do is drive the car, I'll take care of the rest."

His hand shaking, Moses put the car in gear. He had no choice but to do as the reprobate garden gnome bade, for if he displeased Thorax, his mother would remain a statue for all eternity.

The cops had their guns out before the Datsun even came to a stop. When Moses climbed from the vehicle, there was a lot of threats about reaching for the sky, hippie. Smiling at the fuzz and attempting to give off his mellowest vibes, Moses opened the back door.

All of the cops' training was for naught when Thorax jumped out, brandishing the broadsword.

"I have come for the blood of Randy Pendleton, purveyor of fine ladies shoes. This is your choice, sentries, step aside and live, or die by my hand."

That decision was made by a particularly fat cop who pulled his trigger. The bullet went wide and struck the battered Datsun in the trunk. Moses dove beneath the car, Thorax attacked with lightning speed.

There were four cops on the lawn. Thorax rushed the particularly fat one first, who didn't even have time to squeeze off a second shot before the garden gnome lopped off his head, which, thanks to its perfect sphericalness, rolled quite a distance. The second cop, just a kid, got the broadsword raked across his gut. Innards tumbling, steaming, he dropped to his knees, trying to formulate some iconic last words but coming up with nothing but ragged breathing. The third one begged for his life before Awful Tine, the Sword of Might and Forbearance cleaved him in two. His mouth, not realizing that he was already dead, was still talking about his wife and kids as he fell.

The last cop was older, a veteran. Steely gray hair, a set jaw. He smiled a smile that wasn't a smile, drew a bead on Thorax with his .44.

Holding his breath, Moses wondered if his nightmare was just about to end with the shattering of plaster. Sure, there'd be a trial, his mother would permanently be a statue, and he'd have to spend the rest of his life in prison, but he'd be free of Thorax the Thoroughly Miffed's murderous whims.

He needn't have worried. The veteran fired, but the garden gnome was too quick. The bullet struck the ground as Thorax lunged, shouting gibberish curses.

First, the gnome cut off the man's arm that was gripping his weapon. It made a sound like a liquid football as it hit the turf. His eyes wide and begging, the cop started walking backward. A blood waterfall cascading down his side. He backed into a mighty elm, which impeded his progress.

Obviously enjoying himself, Thorax sauntered forward, the sword dragged by his side. "It appears, sentry, that you have come to your end."

The cop could only shake his head.

In one swift move, the garden gnome drove Awful Tine, the Sword of Might and Forbearance deep into the man's chest, pinning him to a tree.

The cop flailed around a bit before quieting.

"Sweet Jesus' balls," cut a voice through the night. Moses looked up to see a man on the porch. Dressed in pajamas. Thin and sweaty.

Flapping his arms like a flightless bird, the man scurried to the nearest police cruiser, marked ARLINGTON PD on the side, which was idling. Desperate, Thorax attempted to pull his sword from the tree, but it held fast. "Help me, Son of Moår, Randy Pendleton, purveyor of fine ladies shoes, is fleeing!"

Before Moses could react, Pendleton threw the car in reverse, backed over the lawn, and disappeared into the night.

WHARF BAR SOCIETY

Giles Moribund had a hard time keeping his voice steady as he ordered a gimlet.

"A what?" the bartender growled. He had thick everything: lips, neck, arms, accent.

Afraid that he'd broken some unwritten rule of wharf bar society, Giles licked his lips and glanced around at his fellow customers. Thugs, prostitutes, professional bowlers. He shuddered and ordered a beer, any beer.

Grunting, the bartender sauntered away.

Under his breath, Giles cursed his *faux pas*. He'd worked hard to blend in at the Sickly Merman Tavern. Wearing his shabbiest Armani shirt, mussing his hair, and dousing himself with a recently acquired bottle of Larry the Cable Guy's cologne, Oh da Toilet, for the occasion. He felt practically homeless.

But all this subterfuge hadn't prevented the thugs and professional bowlers from glaring at him when he entered the establishment. Every nerve in his body was telling him to turn tail and run, but he couldn't.

He was on a mission.

The bartender returned with a mug of flat beer and slopped it down before Giles. Suds everywhere.

"Thank you, my good man," said the former ad exec before he remembered where he was.

Smiling, the Barkeep leaned over and spat an

impressive gobber into the beer, walked away.

Making a mental note to lodge an official complaint with the Better Business Bureau first thing in the morning, Giles felt a hand, large and rough, land upon his shoulder. Wincing, he turned. The man who towered behind him was fit for only two jobs on this earth: professional killer or wall.

In a surprisingly high voice, the man said, "Oh that Henri, you must forgive him. He has overactive salivary glands. This condition makes his life a living hell."

Struggling to form words, Giles said, "You... you must be the man Hussein sent. I'm Giles--"

"Here at the Sickly Merman, we tend to not use our real names."

"Oh," said Giles, catching on. "I'm Miles. Do you have an alias?"

"I have several, but you can call me whatever you wish."

Giles thought about that one for a moment, then named something he truly loved. "I shall call you Asiago."

Showing his rotted teeth, the giant said, "Like the cheese? I like that one, I'm a big fan of dairy. So, I heard you wanted someone dead."

Lowering his voice, leaning forward. "Yes, my daughter, Regan."

A PRICKIFIER, IF YOU WILL

Sitting in his patrol car, Deputy Sheriff Krispy Krowbart absentmindedly played with himself through a sheen of polyester. This action wasn't meant to bring about release, he was just so agitated he was attempting to calm his frayed nerves. Like a baby with a pacifier. A prickifier, if you will.

After arresting a world renowned spokesanimal and tossing him in a cell, Krowbart assumed his life was about to shift from middling to really flipping cool. That he'd reach a level of stardom along the lines of his hero, Larry the Cable Guy.

He pictured himself in the national spotlight: *the man who brought down Tenderbear!* He'd monetize this hullabaloo - a book maybe, a reality TV show of some stripe, one of them coloring books for mentally challenged adults - and buy a bigger trailer, get all sorts of liposuction, and a pair of them fancy slippers made from the souls of dolphins. All of this acclaim would allow him to ditch the current Mrs. Sheriff Krispy Krowbart, sexual wet noodle, and finally obtain his ultimate goal: gaining access to Reba McEntire's greasy mousehole.

Though he'd given it over twenty-four hours, none of this fame junk had unfolded. Instead, he was hounded by the press. They were not painting him a hero for pulling a dangerous spokesanimal off the streets but instead were accusing him of tarnishing one of the country's most beloved institutions.

Stupid liberal media.

At the grocery store, he got mean stares from women, children, and what he could only assume were homosexuals. At home, his wife, who'd always had a cruel streak, stopped cooking his meals and picking up his dirty clothes. She even had the gumption to hire a plumber to come in and replace all his Stars and Bars toilet seats with ones that featured flamingos. This morning, when he sat down to crap, he felt the gay creeping up into his ass cheeks.

Basically, he was trapped in a living hell.

To avoid human contact and the barbs and arrows that went with, the deputy sheriff had gone underground, more or less. No longer did he hang out at the Dew Drop Inn waxing away, or telling tales down at Sumerduck's only barber shop. He was through with people for a while. Visitors were barred from the jail where Allan Krapowitz was being held.

Krowbart himself avoided Krapowitz. He was a creepy flipping dude. Didn't talk, just growled. Wouldn't eat anything but berries and honey, shat in the corner.

Just thinking of Krapowitz sent a chill down the lawman's back as he sat in his patrol car on the warm summer night. Once again he was out on Bluegrass Road, usually the quietest stretch of road in all of Fauquier County. Just trying to make sense of the stars and playing with himself just a little bit.

Happy to be out of the glare of the spotlight, even

for a moment.

But then he heard a sound, a roar. Distant but not for long. Sitting up straight, he spied a car pop over the hill going about 100 miles per hour. As the vehicle flew past him, Krowbart dropped his dick and tried to rub the disbelief out of his eyes. This wasn't just any car, it was an official police vehicle. ARLINGTON PD painted proudly down the side.

The guy behind the wheel definitely was not a cop. He was wearing pajamas, his eyes panicked saucers, his mouth hanging open. Looking over his shoulder as if Old Scratch himself were coming.

Wondering if his eyes were funning him, Krowbart turned on his siren and gave chase yet again.

STILL, DEAD

While Handjob Krapowitz III snored, Regan slipped from the bed and, without putting on her robe, left the bedroom behind.

She crossed to her balcony; dawn was just breaking. Opening the door, she hoped for a gentle summer breeze to caress her body.

But the air was still, dead.

Finding one of the many pink notebooks stashed around her place, she wrote a quick note to Handjob. Picking up her phone, she called for Moribund Advertising's private jet to be fueled and waiting for her on the runway.

HELLO BERSERKER

Harland Harmland drank to forget he was an alcoholic. Since birth, starting with his unfortunate name, nothing had gone right for Harland. He never knew his father though it was rumored that he was a morphine addict. His mother, Morlean, was the fattest woman in Sumerduck, Virginia, which is really saying something. By the age of twelve, the boy was working down in the mud mines to support his mother's Moonpie addiction. Then the mud mines closed when the owners realized there was no money in it. A few weeks later, Morlean choked to death on her first ever salad. That night, Harland Harmland got drunk beyond reason and hadn't been sober since.

Eighty-six years later, he was spending yet another night in the Fauquier County Jail. Once, it had been a nice place to sleep off a drunk. But now that that giant pink bear man had taken up residence across the corridor, the neighborhood had gone to hell. The giant pink bear man didn't make conversation, though Harland had plenty of interesting stories. The creature spent most of his time sleeping.

He was doing so when Deputy Sheriff Krowbart brought in the insane man, who was dressed in pajamas and wouldn't stop babbling. The insane man fought against the cuffs that bound him, twisting this way and that, so he and the deputy sheriff looked as if they were dancing. Shouting at the top of his lungs, "The Sigma Omega Sigma Killer is after me, and he's a magical garden gnome with a giant sword."

"So you've said, Mr. Pendleton," grumbled Krowbart, "about a million times."

"But you gotta believe me, I'm a purveyor of fine ladies shoes."

"Listen, I'll cut you a deal. You act nice and stop talking crazy and I'll make a few inquiring phone calls on your behalf. But you gotta wait in this cell so's you don't do any harm to yourself or others."

The insane man calmed down some and Krowbart helped him into the cell next to the giant pink bear man, who hadn't so much as stirred from his hibernation during this whole kerfuffle.

Slamming the cell door behind him, Krowbart walked away, shaking his head.

The insane man's eyes found Harland looking at him. The old man tried to look away, but he wasn't fast enough. "Hey buddy, you believe me, right? I'm one of those Sigma Omega Sigma brothers that everybody's talking about. University of Illinois, class of 1992. In fact, I'm one of only two left, but that might not be for long. You see, I'm being chased by the devil himself and he's a garden gnome. I gotta get out of here, you gotta help me escape."

It was enough to make Harland consider giving up drinking.

Fortunately, Harland didn't have to formulate a response to the insane man's begging, as, from down the hall, from the offices, came a terrible scream that died in its infancy. Then a thud.

The giant pink bear man stirred.

"See," cried the insane man in a voice so sharp it hurt Harland's ears, "there's the evil garden gnome now and he's coming for my soul!"

Sure enough, a garden gnome came striding down the corridor, but he didn't look like any garden gnome Harland had ever seen. For one thing, he was mobile. For another, he was covered with blood. In one hand, he held a sword that was easily three times as long as he was. In the other, a set of keys. Glistening crimson.

Now the insane man, who was, apparently, not as insane as Harland first assumed, really began to scream in earnest. But Harland knew no one was going to come; there was no one left to save him.

On his short, stubby legs, the gnome took his sweet time reaching the formerly insane man's cell. The purveyor of fine ladies shoes backed away from the bars, as if that was going to do any good.

The bloodied keys jangling dully, the gnome let himself into the cell. Dragging the long sword behind him, sparking on the cement floor.

Blubbering, the man asked, "But why are you doing this? Why are you wiping out the Sigma Omega Sigma brotherhood?"

"Because, awful son of Moår, you wiped out my brotherhood. This is for Longdyke, Viginamouth, Bustybeard the Mediocre, and the rest!"

Grunting, the gnome raised the sword and silver flashed through the air, sharp lightning. Though he wanted to, Harland couldn't look away. The blade, true, tore through the man's torso, ripping flesh. His screams turned to shrieks as he fell to the floor. Laughing, the gnome hacked and hacked and hacked until the man's screams were silenced. Each blow was so forceful that it lifted his tiny body up off the ground. Chunks of pajamaed flesh flew through the air, which was now misted a fine red.

The giant pink bear man made a noise low in his throat that finally drew Harland's attention away from the attack. The creature was standing at the bars of his cage, his nose thrust into the air. From where he stood, he could not see the carnage, but he could certainly smell it.

When he finished hacking the man into bite-sized chunks, the gnome, breathing heavy, came back into the corridor. Along with the sword and the keys, the little man now carried the formerly insane man's head, which still looked terrified. Harland took a step back but the murderer didn't even look his way. He only had eyes for the giant pink bear man.

"Why, hello Berserker, it's been a long time. Do you care none for yon present captivity?"

Shaking his head, the bear growled. Harland could feel that growl in his nuts.

The gnome unlocked its cage and set the giant pink bear man free.

Dragging his weapon, the gnome walked away as the bear walked into the next cage on all fours and devoured what was left of the purveyor of fine lady's shoes.

MACRAMÉ OWLS AND SHIT

She wanted to be like Ed McMahon. Except not fat or dumb or drunk or dead. But Megan did want to show up on Moses Guttchenridder's doorstep and change his life for the better.

But things didn't quite work out as planned.

She showed up on his porch, but he wasn't home. She knocked and knocked but there was no answer. Checking her watch, she saw it was only 7:30 in the morning.

Perhaps he was already at work. Her tiny pink suitcase clutched, Regan walked toward the downtown square of Normal, Iowa, which was only a few blocks away.

The only business open was the Gastrofocker Café, which was hopping. A gaggle of old farmers with their seed caps and dour expressions, a few business people, some students. Regan took the last available seat at the counter, tucked her suitcase beneath her feet. She searched for a menu, but there wasn't one.

Smacking gum, the waitress approached her, order pad and pencil in hand. "Passing through?"

"I'm in town looking for Moses Guttchenridder. Do you know him?"

"It's a small town, sister, everyone knows everyone, knows their business. So, why are you looking for

Moses? Is he in trouble?"

"No, quite the opposite. Why would you assume he was in some kind of trouble?"

The waitress placed the pencil behind her ear, looked out the window at the summer morning stretching its legs. "He's been acting weird of late, old Moses has."

Oh my God, Regan thought, *he is a goat fucker.*

"In... in what way has he been acting weird?" Regan could feel her heart beating unpleasantly in her chest. She thought of the note she'd written to Handjob. Her stomach clenched.

"He's, well, he's just been a bit off," the waitress said, vaguely.

With a lump in her throat, Regan asked where Moses might be found.

The waitress asked, "Have you tried his mother's house, that's where he lives?"

"He lives with his mother?" Regan felt her heart sink a little. "Yeah, I've been there."

"Well, maybe he's at his store, getting ready for the day."

"Oh, he owns his own business. That's a positive." She smiled slightly.

"It would be if the business wasn't so goddamn stupid. It's called Macramania, he sells macramé owls and shit like that."

Regan's wan smile withered on the vine. Macramé. She hadn't even heard that word in decades. She felt sick to her stomach.

Perhaps she was wrong about Moses Guttchenridder. She certainly hoped not, but she also hoped that somehow Handjob had missed the note she'd left, but she doubted that.

THE LAST SIGMA OMEGA SIGMA BROTHER LEFT ALIVE

Handjob Krapowitz III sat at his desk, fuming. Clenching and unclenching his fists, blinking his cataract-bejewleled eyes at an alarming rate, making a tiny injured bird noise deep in his throat.

That morning when he woke in Regan's bed, a stretch of dried cum on his stomach, his lover had already flown the coop.

Picking a chip of jizz from his person and popping it in his mouth for old time's sake, he rose and was surprised to find a note taped to his penis.

He removed said note for comfort's sake, but didn't read it right away, as it was written on pink paper. That wasn't good. Their relationship was not built upon love notes and flowers and boxes of chocolates. It was pleasure-based and that's how Handjob wanted to keep it. If this pink note was gushy, filled with words of love and doodles of arrows cleaving hearts, he would have to drop Regan, despite her nice rack, and find a new fuck buddy.

This unfortunate course of action had happened before, many times. Handjob's joy knob had that affect on the females; they wanted more, they wanted everything.

His hands uncertain, he raised the note, read it.

Within seconds, he knew this was not about arrows or chocolate. It was short and unsweet.

Dear Handjob,
Since it makes me sick, I want our relationship to end, to die a quick and painful death. In the past, you have threatened that if this were to happen, the Moribund Agency's relationship with KrapKo would suffer. I do not actually believe you would stoop so low. So long, I'll see you this afternoon, professionally, when I return from Iowa with Moses Guttchenridder, the new face of Krap-Wad toilet paper.

She hadn't signed her name, but he knew who it was from.

Mindful of his sciatica, Handjob ripped the note to shreds and tossed them into the air. An indoor, pink snowstorm. Then, for good measure, he pissed on the shreds of paper. Still not satisfied, he shat upon them, which took some time. When he ducked into the bathroom to wipe his ass, he was horrified to discover that Regan didn't even stock Krap-Wad toilet paper, but the leading brand. America's #1 toilet paper: KrapMoore.

It was then Handjob knew exactly what he had to do.

Sitting at the desk in his office, he unclenched his fists and buzzed his secretary to come in.

His secretary, an old woman named Margarine Butterfield, was as ugly as hell. Flabby in all the wrong places, gray hair, thick glasses. Every day she wore a muumuu and her dentures needed to be powerwashed. Handjob had hired her in hopes that he wouldn't fuck her, as he had done with all his previous secretaries. That had caused some problems on the homefront with Mrs. Krapowitz.

Unfortunately, there was that one regrettable time when, drunk, he'd accidentally wandered into the copy room and found Margarine Butterfield hovering by the Xerox. Something about the way she caressed the platen made him horny. Threatening her with unemployment, he forced her to take her dentures out so that she could administer the mother of all hummers.

The next day, he'd apologized for his dick's indiscretion with a ten cents an hour raise and a family pack of Krap-Wad toilet paper. But, to this day, she regarded him coldly.

He wanted to fire her but was afraid of a lawsuit over the forced blowjob incident. One really had to watch their P's and Q's in these politically correct times. So, he kept her around, praying that she would simply expire one day soon.

As Margarine entered his office, she said glumly, "You rang?"

"Get me the singing telegram people, I've got--"

"Did you hear that the Sigma Omega Sigma Killer has struck again?"

He blanched. "Randall Pendleton..."

Drawing a finger across her fleshy wattle, she said, "Murdered down in some shitty berg in Virginia."

"Head missing?"

She nodded with glee as he searched the desk for

his flask. When he found it, he drained half of it in one ferocious gulp. "Why do you take such enjoyment from these deaths?"

"Cause they're interesting. You want to know what else is interesting? Pendleton was killed in the same jail where they were holding Tenderbear."

"What? Why was Pendleton incarcerated?"

She shrugged. "And Tenderbear's gone missing."

"Missing?"

"Missing. All they found was a set of bloody paw prints heading off into the woods."

This prompted Handjob to polish off the flask. "This is terrible, simply terrible. You're aware of what this means, of course?"

Smiling her mossy dentures, she said, "That you're the last Sigma Omega Sigma brother left alive, Crappy."

WEIRDLY LARGE COLLECTION OF MOUNTED ANIMAL PENISES

It had not been a good twenty-four hours for Quentin Quartermaster, Regan Moribund's assistant.

The previous evening, he'd showed up at Chaps in Chaps, his favorite gay bar in all of New York, in his most fabulous chaps. They were made from leather with faux purple fur piping. Really accentuated his bulge.

Although he struck up a few interesting conversations with some very nice, very hunky English dudes, nothing came of it. No sex. Not even a peck on the cheek.

Insult to injury, when he returned home to his tiny studio in the most dangerous and unmentionable neighborhood in New York, Bludgeonburg, he found some cad had broken in and stolen his collection of Menudo memorabilia.

All night he cried and cried, dampening his fabulous chaps. The following morning work was even more of a nightmare than usual.

He'd heard whispers that Regan was about to be put out on her liposuctioned-ass by her father, but those rumors turned out to be ass-backwards.

Now Regan had the corner office and Quentin found it nearly impossible to keep his composure in the face of such horror.

Since the moment he met Regan, at his job interview,

he hated her. Her smugness, her pettiness, the way she got any man she desired and Quentin had to work to get the ugly ones.

It was so unfair!

And now that she was queen of Moribund Advertising, the world was her sexual oyster.

This aggression would not stand.

While she was out of town on business, Quentin unpacked Regan's weirdly large collection of mounted animal penises and put them around her new office in what he hoped was an anti-feng shui fashion. During this labor, he made a vow to himself.

He would bring down Regan Moribund if it was the last thing he ever did.

BREATHING THE AIR OF FREEDOM

Throughout the day, Tenderbear made his way north. Sticking to the woods, eating whatever berries and dead animals he could find along the way. Breathing the air of freedom, feeling the gentle summer breeze upon his fur.

THE JAMES EARL JONES OF ASSES

No response.

Once again and a little harder, Regan knocked on the glass door of Macramania. Nothing, no sound, no movement. Cupping her hands, she pressed her face against the mucky glass and peered deep into the store. The space was small and crammed with what could only be described as crap: macramé owls with wooden eyes; hideous, misshapen pottery and wicker. Tons and tons of wicker. More wicker than a human would ever have call for in an entire lifetime. Everything covered with a fine patina of dust. It looked more like a junk shop than anything else.

Regan's heart sank all the way down to the soles of her pink Manolo Blahniks. She never cried, it was a sign of weakness, but she could feel tears gathering. *What the fuck was she doing? What kind of stupid plan had she hatched? Pulling a spokesperson from the White Pages of some shitass town in the middle of nowhere? No market research, no focus groups? She might as well have suggested a talking ass being the new spokesthing from Krap-Wad toilet paper.*

That thought stopped the tears from advancing.

A talking ass... that might not be so bad... if it had the right voice... something soothing... like James Earl Jones... yes, the James Earl Jones of asses... it was worth thinking about... could save her career...

Of course, there was also that sticky problem concerning the toxic note that she had left attached to Handjob Krapowitz III's minuscule love knob.

Regan had to act and act quickly to stop the avalanche she'd started. She had to get back to civilization and put things right.

Spinning on her heels to start the journey back to the tiny Normal Airport, she gasped when she spied the most handsome man she'd ever seen standing right behind her.

Holding an incredibly life-like garden gnome in the crook of his arm.

A KIND FACE AND AN EVEN KINDER RACK

Climbing crusty from the Datsun, in which he'd spent far too many hours, Moses was surprised to find a customer waiting outside Macramania. A customer he'd never seen before. In fact, he'd never seen this beautiful woman anywhere around Normal; he definitely would have remembered her. She was beyond beautiful, she was heart-stopping. The type that deserved canvases and poems written in blood. She was tall, thin, had raven hair that caught the gentle summer wind just so. She had a kind face and an even kinder rack.

Her beauty was so unsettling that Moses nearly dropped Thorax the Thoroughly Miffed, whom he'd told to remain perfectly still.

"Oh, hey there, yeah, are you like waiting for Macramania to open?" He tried to check his watch then remembered that he didn't wear one, never had.

"Are you Moses Guttchenridder?"

This stranger, who was all business, knew his name and spoke in a flat tone. That was bad, very bad. His smile froze, melted.

The FBI. That's who this woman was, despite all the pink she was wearing and the marvelous rack. Obviously she worked on the Sigma Omega Sigma Killer task force and had tracked him down.

She was probably going to shoot him with a pink gun crammed with pink bullets.

"That... that depends on who's asking," he croaked. Moses looked around wildly, searching for an escape route. Were there more Feds secreted around the town square? Was he surrounded? Should he just give up or make a run for it? Go down in a hail of bullets? End this misery?

She furrowed her brow. Even confused, she was beautiful. "I'm Regan Moribund, I work for KrapKo, we spoke on the phone yesterday."

Relief washed over him; he was probably not about to be shot. "Oh, yeah, right... but you live in New York City."

"I do. I also own a private jet. I fully realize that you told me yesterday that you were not interested in becoming the spokesperson for Krap-Wad toilet paper, but I just wanted to talk to you in person to see if I could change your mind."

"It's changed," he blurted before he could think. Although he was right there in his arms, Moses had forgotten about the homicidal garden gnome. "I'll do it. I'll do anything you ask."

ASIAGO PRESSATO

To celebrate his new name, Asiago the hitman bought a pound of *asiago pressato* at the local deli and ate it while he waited outside Regan Moribund's building. He sat there for hours, nibbling, sighing in contentment, and looking out for the young woman he was going to kill.

SCREAMING MOUTHGASM

Gastrofocker's Café had cleared out some and now there were tables available, but Moses still preferred to sit at the counter.

"I'm starving," Regan confessed, "I was here an hour ago but I didn't eat. There were no menus and that scared me, so I just had some coffee."

"Oh, the coffee's awesome here, isn't it?"

It was, surprisingly so, and Regan told Moses as much, staring into the pools of his blue eyes, wishing that she'd brought her bathing suit.

Moses explained, "François grows his own coffee beans right out back."

"Who's François?"

"François Gastrofocker, he owns this place. He's from Marseille, in France. He used to operate an ice cream truck business there but he ran afoul of the powerful Marseille ice cream truck mafia. After one of his drivers was bludgeoned to death, he moved to Normal, Iowa, where he could cook in peace. There are no menus because François doesn't believe in borders. He can cook you anything you want, at any time."

She could actually feel her leg being pulled. "Anything?"

For the first time in her presence, he smiled. It

looked like lightning that tasted like sugar. "Anything."

When the chatty waitress came around, Regan, wanting to put Moses' assertion to the test, ordered *cuisses de genoville*. The waitress just stared at her, slack jawed. Regan felt like she'd won some secret bet.

"Frog legs, Flo" Moses interjected, interpreting.

"Oh them," said the waitress, scribbling on her order pad.

Moses ordered some *nam tok moo* and a Coke. Flo waddled off.

Unable to keep from grinning, Regan asked what the hell *nam tok moo* was.

"It's a Thai pork dish," Moses replied, rubbing his eyes and stifling a yawn.

She put her hand on his arm and felt a current flow between their bodies. If this is what it felt like to be electrocuted, she longed to be sent to the chair. "You look exhausted."

"Yeah, I am. I was up all night."

"Why?"

"I... I just couldn't sleep. I was so excited by your offer."

"But... but you turned me down."

"Oh look, our food's here."

"But we just ordered--"

Regan nearly fainted when she turned to see the waitress shuffling their way with two plates held high. Steam rising. One was piled precariously with frog legs, the other some dark meat in a murky juice.

Without ceremony, the waitress dropped the plates before the couple.

For a moment Regan was too surprised to take a bite but Moses tucked in as if he had not eaten for days.

Mentally shrugging, she took a tentative bite and experienced a screaming mouthgasm.

"Oh my God," she moaned, breaking the rule about not talking with one's mouth full. "This is so fucking good."

"It is, but honestly I prefer François' *congee*."

She took another bite, a big one. Gesturing with a frog leg bone, she had to ask, "So, the gnome... what's up with him exactly?"

He'd carried the lawn ornament all the way from his shop, and placed it gently on the counter of the café when they sat.

"Oh, Thorax? He's just... he's just always around."

DRIED BLOOD MUSTACHE

There were many things that Violet Verp hated about her life. There was her house, which was isolated, cramped and smelled like a gym bag filled with fetid bacon. There was her husband, Brutwire, who never bothered to wash the grit from his hands before he grabbed her coarsely and threw her down upon the nearest piece of furniture. There was her furniture, which was all stained. There was her army of offspring, all snot and attitude.

There was the continuous, monotonous, list of chores that consumed her days. The dirty floors, always caked with jam, the cooking for seven bellies that never seemed to reach capacity, and the laundry, a never-ending mountain of filthy clothes.

Sighing about her lot in life, Violet Verp stood in her backyard in rural Rickshaw, New Jersey, hanging laundry on the line. She was thinking about running away.

She didn't want to run far. Just to the nearest bridge and fling herself into the cold waters of the Passaic River. Let the gentle waters drag her under.

Every night, usually while her husband grunted atop her, she prayed to Jesus Christ, the Savior, to deliver upon her some inoperable cancer or let her be smashed flat by a semi.

Behind her, near the tree line, a noise. The snap of a twig. Dropping one of Brutwire Jr's NASCAR jerseys, she spun.

Standing not ten feet away was Tenderbear. But not the cute, lovable Tenderbear from the airwaves. This one was dirty, its pink fur matted. It had a dried blood mustache. His sailor cap., usually cocked at a jaunty angle, was now barely clinging to the side of his head.

But she wasn't afraid.

This is what she'd been praying for.

Hands shaking, she beckoned the bear towards her.

Tenderbear moved with surprising speed. He was upon her, had her pinned to the ground, before she could make a sound. As his sharp teeth ripped into Violet's white fleshy neck, she thought: Thank you, Jesus, thank...

CLOUDS OF JIZZ

Her nipples were as pink as her outfit. Perfect and pert. Friendly and inviting, like miniature, round welcome mats. Moses licked them, flicked them, and stared at them long enough to be able to pick them out in a police line-up.

Standing and looking him right in the eye as if she had nothing to hide, everything to share, Regan pulled down her skirt. There was nothing underneath. Well, genitalia, of course, which, no shocker here, was pink.

Spreading her ass cheeks, she bent over. Barely able to breathe, much less stand, Moses got to his pegs and gently rammed his throbbing knob deep into this strange, amazing woman who'd blown into his life only hours before, changing it for the better, like a sexier, less dead, Ed McMahon.

Sure, he'd had a handful of Normal girls before, but that's exactly what they were: normal. Missionary position, usually at night and always in the bedroom. Now here he was, getting his rocks off in the middle of the living room, in the middle of the day, with the most beautiful woman he'd ever laid eyes on.

He was in love so deep he feared he never find his way out again.

They'd spent the entire day together, every second.

Even when she had to pee, she'd made him watch. After a delicious meal at Gastrofocker's Café, he'd shown her the highlights of Normal, which had taken ten minutes or so. In the square was the statue of Ekim Sinrut, the man who'd founded Normal 133 years prior. He'd shown her Macramania and she seemed genuinely interested in his vast wicker collection (of course, he didn't dare tell her Macramania was really just a front; he sold weed out of the backroom and made a fortune). On the walk to show her the pavilion in Chautauqua Park, she'd reached over and taken his hand. Something sweeter than lightning burrowed through his body and found his genitalia. Since walking and erections don't go hand-in-hand, he found a bench where they could sit and talk about their diverse childhoods. Never once did he let go of her hand. In fact, he promised himself he would never let go of her, even if she were on fire.

When things died down dick-wise, they continued their journey to the Chautauqua Pavilion, under which they shared their first kiss. Moses' hard-on returned and, as the kisses grew longer and deeper, it unpacked its bags right in his pants.

With any other woman, he would have died of embarrassment about the sticky stain spreading its wings beneath his belt. But not with Regan. She just giggled lightly and got down on her knees right out there in front of God and everybody, in the place where the Guttchenridder family had held many family picnics, and undoing his pants, she licked him clean. Took her time doing it too.

Fearing that ejaculate was about to shoot from his every pore, he groaned, grabbed her and practically dragged her to his house. Nearly leaving Thorax, who was doing a great job pretending to be a statue, behind.

Though Moses could tell he was pissed.

As they stopped on his porch for another round of kisses, he realized that he loved this woman, and he wanted to share his life with her. Well, everything except the secrets that he kept down in his basement.

Fucking her from behind, right there on the living room floor, beneath a portrait of his mother that he'd painted in high school, with Thorax stiffly watching from the shadows, Moses blew his wad yet again. This time Regan came with him, shouting and writhing as if she were on fire. Still conjoined, they fell to the wooden floor. There would be bruises. He held her tight, kept her close, as he became flaccid and fell out of her tufted treasure. Kissing every part of her. Sometimes gently, other times with bad intent.

Licking a globule of sweat from the downy hairs that decorated his taint, Regan said, "Moses, darling, I have a confession to make."

Caressing her perfect ass, he said, "Whatever you've done, dearest, it matters not to me."

After wetting her finger, she massaged his bunghole and said, "Oh love, I fear I haven't been the best person."

When she entered him, Moses winced. "Whatever it is will not lessen the love I feel for you, sweetheart."

Removing her finger, she sucked on his velvet orbs for a moment before stuffing them into her love trench. "But I'm afraid I've been something of a trollop. Sad to say, I've had many, many men."

"I simply don't believe a word of it, my treasure," he said, ejaculating again. As clouds of jizz flew through the air, she caught them in her mouth like popcorn.

Spitting his pearl jam into her hand and massaging it into her clit, she said, "As much as it pains me to admit, dear one, it is the God's honest truth."

"I don't care, beloved, you can have as many lovers as you please." He polished his penguin while watching her climax yet again. Shouting endearments, Regan squirted all over the floor.

While he lapped the puddle of her ejaculate from the wooden floor, she ruffled his hair and said, "That's not what I want, my little donut, for you are the only man for me now."

"And you are the only woman for me." Still hard, he buried himself as deep into her rusty washer as he could. "But I fear I almost must confess that I too have a terrible secret."

CHAPS IN CHAPS

When all the *asiago pressato* cheese had been consumed, the killer grew bored. He decided to have a little friendly tête-à-tête with the doorman of Regan Moribund's building.

After breaking three of the man's ribs, Asiago introduced himself.

"Like the cheese?" asked the doorman from the floor of the vestibule, though one of his lungs was punctured.

Asiago hit him again. After being cramped in his car all day, he longed for exercise. "I need some information about Regan Moribund."

"Well... she's kind of a whore."

"No, I want to know where she is."

Wheezing, "I don't... I don't know. She took a cab to the airport early this morning."

Another punch. This one was square in the nards. "Where was she headed?"

"That... that I don't know. You'd have to talk to her assistant, Quentin Quartermaster."

"And where might I find this Quartermaster fellow?"

"Well, he likes to hang out at Chaps in Chaps. It's a gay leather club for Englishmen."

"Thanks for the info," said the hitman right before he stomped the man to death.

As he walked away, he said over his shoulder to the cooling corpse, "And yes, my name is Asiago like the cheese."

A PAIR OF BROWN EYES

There was a pair of brown eyes waiting for Giles Moribund when he entered the bedroom of his beloved timeshare condo in Passaic. This brought a smile to his worried face. He'd given the pair of whores very specific instructions on the phone. They were to strip, shut the fuck up, get on the bed, stick their asses high in the air, and wait.

Everything was coming up roses.

At this very moment, back in New York, if things were going as planned, Asiago was smashing the smile off his daughter's stupid face.

Regan's murder could never be pinned on him, he had the perfect alibi. He was out in the wilds of New Jersey getting his anal on with two overpaid hookers.

"Sorry Regan, you're family, but this is a family business," said Giles, under his breath, walking toward the bed, peeling off his suit, his erection flourishing.

"What?" asked the dark-haired whore.

Since he needed her testimony later, Giles couldn't smack the shit out of her, which is what he felt like doing, he could only reprimand her and remind her to keep her mouth shut.

To punish her, he sprang upon the bed and entered her back slit without a word of warning, thrusting as hard as his tiny old body could muster.

"When in the Course of human events, it becomes necessary for one people to dissolve the political bands which have connected them with another..."

She screamed, he smiled. Pumping away, he heard a sound outside the condo. A deep growling, like a bear. He stopped thrusting, cocked his head, listened. Branches breaking, something large was moving through the woods. But that was impossible. He was in the middle of New Jersey, the only wild animals they had out here were Italians.

But something made him disengage, forget the Declaration of Independence, climb from the bed, cross to the window, and look out into the night. It was pitch black, no moon, but he could still make out a sliver of pink, just beyond the children's play area, near the woods.

He whispered, "Tenderbear..."

"What'd you just say?" the dark-haired one piped up again. She was now sitting on the bed, drawing a cigarette from her bag. Giles made a mental note to have Asiago take care of her after she served her purpose.

"Get your ass back up in the air and shut the fuck up. I'll be back in a few minutes."

WATCHING OPRAH

Looking deep into Regan's eyes, Moses sat on the toilet and desperately tried to take a shit. Nothing. Not even a wet fart. Dropping his head, "I feel like such a fraud. You want me to sell toilet paper and I haven't had a decent bowel movement in a month. That's my dirty secret."

Regan left her place in the doorway and came forward. Naked and beautiful. She laid a cooling hand upon Moses' face, wiping away some sweat. "Oh darling, I think I have just the thing for that."

"I've tried everything. Laxatives, drinking tons of coffee, watching Oprah."

"What I have in mind always works. And, to boot, it's tons of fun."

She had forgotten to pack her bathing suit, but she never went anywhere, even the grocery store, without her giant pink strap-on.

NO BODY, NO BONES, NO BLOOD

No one could accuse the Chaps in Chaps of false advertising.

Even though the night was cooling, there was a long line of young men, all wearing nothing but chaps, drinking tea, talking soccer, waiting their turn to enter the club.

Not a big fan of waiting, Asiago cut the line and gained admittance by cupping his giant hand over the bouncer's scared face and squeezing real hard.

Inside, disco ruled and dudes were dancing and kissing and groping. The scene turned Asiago's stomach. He may have been a professional killer, but he was raised Catholic and this gay business weighed upon his soul something fierce.

After asking around – breaking up some passionate pairings and busting a few heads – Asiago found Quentin Quartermaster in the bathroom, getting his dick sucked by a young man who was wearing nothing but a pair of fairy wings.

"How unfuckingimaginative," said the hitman.

"Hey, do you mind?" asked Quartermaster. "This is the first action I've had in months."

"And it's the last you'll ever have," declared the hitman.

Grabbing the cocksucker by the nape of his

scrawny neck and hurling him with all his might. The fairy hit the wall with such force that he simply disappeared. No body, no bones, no blood. Just a cloud of sparkly dust, which flitted to the ground to the sound of harp music.

"Holy shit," said Quartermaster, duly impressed.

Although he was deeply shocked by the fairy implosion, Asiago tried to sound calm as he asked, "Are you Quentin Quartermaster?"

The young man nodded stupidly and Asiago didn't even give him a chance to stuff himself back in his white leather chaps that were Bedazzled within an inch of their lives before dragging him out of the club.

THE TALE OF HOW THEY BECAME SO DEAD

Never before had Moses been on the receiving end of a really good fuck, Regan working that pink strap-on like a magic wand, and he found that he quite enjoyed the experience. After blowing his wad, he had to scoot to the bathroom to have a really nice shit. He couldn't get the grin off his face as he wiped his ass with Krap-Wad toilet paper and imagined himself hawking their product on national TV.

He even pictured himself wearing that sailor cap. at a jaunty angle and saying, "My bottom feels like it's back on top!"

Racing to his bedroom, he called, "Hey Regan, dude, I've been totally rethinking the whole sailor cap issue and--"

In the doorway, he stopped, froze. As expected, Regan was sprawled on the bed, naked, glistening, her rack glorious, waiting. It was the look on her face that punched Moses square in the solar plexus. Eyes bulging, her mouth curled into a rictus sneer, she was staring into the dark corner of the room.

Stepping into the light, Thorax said, "I appears, Son of Moår, that you have not informed yonder womanfolk of my existence."

Absorbed with love and fucking, Moses had been kidding himself, putting off the inevitable. Of course if he wanted Regan in his life, she would have to find out about the murderous garden gnome. Thinking these two would not cross paths was like falling off a skyscraper and expecting to not hit the ground.

But Moses wasn't prepared for this moment. Just stood there, shaking his head ever so slightly, his mouth as open as a wound.

As if she were just learning the language, Regan spoke slowly, "Moses, what... what the hell... is this some kind of sick joke?"

"Oh fair maiden with the glorious rack, there be definite sickness but no humor in this situation. But if the spy of me leaves you so flastered, wait 'til ye see what yon son of Moår has down in his base-ment."

There was no stopping her. Moses tried, in vain, to grab Regan as she flew passed him, strap-on flopping like a crazed snake, pushing him aside, but the only thing he caught was a sniff of her: sex and latex. He wanted to explain, though there was no explanation. He heard her footsteps, harsh and retreating.

"It seems, son of Moår, that yon ladyfriend is a little miffed herself. It be best if ye be there when the wench finds out what we've been up to for the last month."

On legs newborn and faulty, Moses spun and followed Regan. He would never catch her, could never catch her, as she was gone like a hurricane, blustery and busy.

There was a scream from somewhere deep in the bowels of the house.

He found her in the basement, standing in the middle of the earthen floor as if she'd never move again. She was staring at the frozen statue of Moses' mother, Helen. Wearing an apron and a look of complete surprise. Helen was standing near the furnace, where she had been for weeks; Moses dusting her every other day.

Without turning around, Regan asked, "Is that your mother?"

"Yes."

"You have her eyes. Is she dead?"

"No, the bummer of a garden gnome put her in a state of suspended animation, keeping her hostage basically, until we finish his task."

"I take it that his task has something to do with all the heads?"

Beyond his mother was a field of heads. Mounted on pikes that were driven into the ground, a macabre chessboard.

When they'd started their killing spree, Moses had begged Thorax to not take the heads of the victims as trophies, but the gnome would have none of that noise.

Though she had her back to him, Moses could tell that Regan was crying. "Who... who do these heads belong to?"

His mind blurred, cracked. There was no lie that could fix things now. Moses was in far too deep and the only way to gain freedom was to tell the truth. Regan deserved as much, even if that meant she would flee and the police would show up. Even as he was being pumped full of bullets, he knew he'd be thankful for this beautiful day, for his time with Regan, for her smile, her laugh, and the amazing way that she fucked him in the ass.

But before he could explain, Thorax piped up. Moses hadn't even heard him coming down the stairs. "Those, lass, are the heads of the worst Sons of Moår to ever walk Arth. Would ye like to hear the tale of how they became so dead?"

Regan turned, tears moistening her glorious rack, and nodded.

ANOTHER BRIEF BURST OF HISTORY

Many years before the Indians came across the land bridge, North America was the land of my people, a brave race of noble gnomes. It is true that we spent most our time warring over land or livestock or shoeware, but that doesn't make us bad people.

One day, a great storm swept over the land. Upon this ill wind came the sound of a harp. Quickly, we gathered our armaments to battle whatever evil was coming.

The clouds parted and down floated a creature the likes of which none of us had ever seen. He was tall and naked, with a pair of wings.

He told us his name was Bernard and he was there to punish us for our war-like ways. Before any of us could fire a single arrow or insult, Bernard flicked his wrist and froze us all right where we stood. At that moment, my race became, basically, tiny statues.

Things really went to hell, as they often do, when the white people showed up. They found us charming. Painting us bright colors, they displayed us in their gardens as decorations. Then, as if things could not get worse, came *Plasternacht*. In 1992, in Champaign, the brothers of Sigma Omega Sigma at the University of Illinois got drunk and decided to drive around town, destroying garden gnomes. Just for giggles. Over a hundred of my brothers died that night and I swore revenge. Obviously, I could do nothing in my deanimated state. Many years passed in torture. But then Bernard showed up again. He'd heard my silent pleas and, saddened by my loss, granted me a reprieve from my curse. He told me I would be released from my frozen state and have one moon's time to seek my revenge. Of course, thanks to my diminutive stature, I had to seek assistance in this matter. The Sigma Omega Sigma brothers had scattered to the four corners, but I couldn't board a plane or bus, couldn't even operate a motor vehicle. I chose Moses Guttchenridder as my human helper based solely on the fact that he possessed me at that time. Over the last thirty days I've wished many times that I'd chosen better, for Moses doesn't care much for blood or violence, and he is not a very good driver.

A SMOTHERING BLANKET

Looking back and forth between the man she had so recently fucked and the gnome, the strap-on wagging like a tail, Regan couldn't believe her eyes or her ears or her anything.

Moses broke the silence that had settled over the basement like a smothering blanket. "I'm not really that bad of a driver, he just likes to go fast and I think safety--"

"That's what you have to say for yourself? You've been an accomplice in over sixty murders. These heads were once people. They had wives, children, friends, fancy shoe shoppes."

Spying a framed picture hanging on the opposite wall, Regan crossed. It was an official photo, taken back in 1992, of the Sigma Omega Sigma brothers gathered on the front porch of their fraternity house. All of them, save one, had black X's slashed across their faces.

Studying the photo closely, Regan felt all the blood in her veins flow backwards. Her hand shaking, she pointed toward the only un-X'ed out face. "This... this is Handjob Krapowitz III."

Moses took a step toward Regan, which made her jump. "Do you know him?"

Upstairs, Moses' doorbell rang in a very official manner.

THE FURRY FACE OF KRAP-WAD TOILET PAPER

"Hello, my son, you've come to speak with me." His hands out before him, Giles Moribund crept toward Tenderbear slowly. He didn't want to scare him.

The giant pink bear didn't move, didn't make a sound. Studied Giles with dull, plastic eyes as he drew closer.

"I have missed you, son. Things went bad for both of us, but they're about to get better. Regan, that bitch, is dead or dying. After the funeral, I will return to my rightful place at the helm of Moribund Advertising, and once again you will be the furry face of Krap-Wad toilet paper and I'll get all the anal I can handle and--"

Uncoiling like a spring, Tenderbear leapt through the night, roaring.

Giles, still smiling, was dead before he hit the ground.

HER ASS IN THE AIR

"Did you hear something?" asked the dark-haired whore.

The other one, the blonde, nodded.

"What do you think it was?"

The blonde shrugged. It wasn't her business what was happening outside. She'd been told to stick her ass in the air and be quiet, and that's what she planned to do.

GOODBYE TO MY DICK, YOU BITCH

When he was young, Glance Bowland dreamed of Broadway. But five struggle-filled years in New York had taught him his dream was a nightmare. With his tail between his legs, he returned to Des Moines, moved into his mother's basement, and took a job with the Good News! Singing Telegram Company. It was embarrassing, but it paid the bills and allowed him to use his beautiful singing voice for something other than entertaining his mother's parakeets.

The assignment he was currently on was a real head-scratcher. Drive all the way out to the shitty little berg of Normal and fire someone via song. This was a new one to Glance, who usually did birthday parties or marriage proposals or lynchings.

He wasn't particularly wild about this assignment, but KrapKo was paying him five hundred dollars – more than double the usual fee – and Glance needed cash, as he was thinking about getting his own place, tired of battling the fucking parakeets for his mother's attention.

His preconceived notions of small town Iowa were shattered when the door was opened by a naked couple. The woman was wearing a pink strap-on.

Assuming that he was on some hidden camera show, which meant he had another shot at stardom,

Glance launched into his song:

>*Hey Regan, you really fucked up*
>*And now you're out the door*
>*You won't be wiping your ass*
>*With Krap-Wad no more*
>*You're fired, you're through, you're done*
>*Now drive into a fucking ditch*
>*For this is Handjob Krapowitz III*
>*So say goodbye to my dick, you bitch.*

EVER THE SECRETARY

While giving him another denture-less hummer, Margarine Butterfield fantasized about biting Handjob Krapowitz III's dick off. His screams, bright, filling the air. The gush of warm blood over her throat, her dress, her life.

But this was just a fantasy; she needed her job at KrapKo, for their insurance covered her husband's chemotherapy.

Fortunately, before he blew his disgusting wad again, the phone on his desk rang. Ever the secretary, Margarine put her teeth back in and answered it.

It was Regan Moribund, she was crying. When Margarine informed her boss of this, he grinned his snaky grin.

Grabbing the phone from her, Handjob shooed Margarine out of his office. She waddled toward the door but hung back to eavesdrop.

"Well Regan, I can tell by your tears that you've gotten the singing telegram... No, I haven't told the board of my decision, we're meeting first thing Monday morning, I'll tell them then... Okay, we can meet, but even if you fuck me, it's not going to change anything."

Slamming the phone down, shattering it, Handjob spied Margarine lurking by the door. "Oh good, you're still here. Regan Moribund will be at my penthouse in four hours. My wife is out of town at one of her ridiculous rind conventions and I want Regan to walk in on me having sex with someone. On such short notice, I'm afraid that's going to have to be you."

DOODLES

The sex was so much better than he'd hoped.

When Asiago first got Quentin Quartermaster back to his apartment, he couldn't wait to kill the little gaywad. Which would happen as soon as he got all the information he needed.

To cover the sound of the beating that he was about to inflict, Asiago had turned on his TV and *Terms of Endearment* was on and one thing led to another and pretty soon Asiago and Quentin were having sex on the couch and cuddling and talking about a long and happy future together.

Quartermaster was a gentle, caring lover. Never before had Asiago been so caressed, so loved. Usually he had to pay for sex, which left him satisfied but cold.

This young man was brimming with tricks and turns. Asiago had screaming orgasm after screaming orgasm.

Worn out, Quartermaster lay next to him. Asiago stroked his hair gently and wondered if this was what love felt like.

"Asiago isn't my real name," the hitman confessed.

"I didn't think so, love."

"It's the name of a cheese."

"I know."

"My real name is Doodles."

Getting up on an elbow, Quentin looked him dead

in the eye. "Doodles, really? That sounds like just another alias."

"It's not. I would never lie to you. My father named me. He was an artist, but not a very good one."

Quentin's cell phone, which was resting on the coffee table, rang. As he reached for it, Asiago kissed the back of his neck, reached around and tweaked his nipple.

Checking the caller ID, Quentin said, "It's her."

The small part of the killer's mind that was still on the clock flamed. "Answer it. Find out what her plans are, when she's coming back to New York."

Nodding, the young man answered. Asiago could hear the woman on the other end of the line. Ranting, raving, swearing. Quentin, lovely Quentin could barely get a word in edgewise with his beautiful thick lips.

No wonder her father wanted her dead.

After he hung up, Quentin said, "She'll be at Handjob Krapowitz's penthouse in four hours."

"Four hours," said Asiago, "that gives us plenty of time."

He dove in, again and again.

ESPECIALLY THE PART ABOUT
THE KILLING

"I don't really understand," said Moses. As Regan had commanded, he was driving the three of them to the Normal airport as fast as he could. "You really changed your tune after that singing telegram."

In the basement, surrounded by heads, she was all you're-going-to-jail-forever and stuff, but after the singing telegram guy, who had a terrible voice, informed her that she was fired, she made a quick call in the next room and was then all grab-your-murderous-gnome-and-let's-get-to-New-York.

The passenger window down, the wind ripping her hair, Regan smiled at Moses. "Everybody has to have a hobby."

"So, suddenly, you're cool with all the killing?"

"Well, I'm a firm believer in finishing what you start and Handjob will be your last one, forever, right, my love?"

From the backseat, Thorax piped up. "Can ye not spy, son of Moår, the man we must kill is Handjob Krapowitz III, the same man who runs KrapKo, the same man who was mentioned in the sex saga sung by the young troubadour."

Moses hung his head as much as he could and still keep an eye on the road. "I thought that was a gnarly coincidence."

Thorax said, "There are times when I fear for ye brains."

Moses looked at Regan. "So, the dude we're going to kill is your boss..."

"Former boss."

He gulped. "And did you two... did you... you know, like, did you dudes ever..."

Rolling her eyes, Regan, "The singing telegram did mention me sucking his dick, so, the answer to your unasked questions is: yes, we were lovers."

The Datsun became engulfed in silence. The only sounds: wind and the gnome sharpening Awful Tine, the Sword of Might and Forbearance in the backseat.

Reaching out, Regan grabbed Moses' knee. "But that was yesterday. From now on, it's just you and me, I promise."

She nuzzled his neck, dismantling his frown.

After kissing Moses several times, Regan said, "So, we'll go to New York, kill that asshole Krapowitz before he meets with the board, I'll get to keep my job, and you'll be the new spokesperson for Krap-Wad toilet paper. Everyone wins."

"Sounds good," said Moses.

"Especially," said Thorax, "the part about killing."

STUPID BIG FUCKER

Stupidbigfuckerstupidbigfuckerstupidbigfucker...

This refrain streamed through Quentin Quartermaster's mind as Asiago guided his big black car through the nighttime traffic of Manhattan.

They pointed out their favorite restaurants, parks where they liked to jog, beloved bars. Eventually they discussed, giggling, what they were going to name their children.

Quentin's stomach flipped, then flopped. But this turmoil didn't show on his face. As Regan Moribund's assistant, he was used to living lies, playing the nice guy. He smiled and played along, held hands with Doodles.

All the time thinking: *stupidbigfuckerstupidbigfucker...*

From the moment Asiago had murdered that beautiful young thing in the bathroom of Chaps in Chaps, Quentin knew he was going to kill the brute. He was just waiting for the right moment, an opening. When Asiago came blubbering to him after that awful scene in *Terms of Endearment* where Shirley MacLaine guts the postman and has sex with his rotting corpse, Quentin gave in to him, kissed him, had sex with him again and again. Quentin had finally found his angle: through Asiago's heart. Or, rather, dick.

Now the young man had a plan. He was going to lead Asiago straight to Regan Moribund then, just as this ape

– who had a surprisingly small penis – was about to kill her, Quentin would jump in and save the day, killing Asiago. That way he could be a hero in the eyes of his stupid bitch boss and get revenge at the same time.

There was only one flaw with this plan: Quentin had no idea how he was going to stop this mansion of a man.

Stupidbigfuckerstupidbigfuckerstupidbigfucker...

THE MILE HIGH CLUB

After Moses joined the Mile High Club for the third time in as many hours, he lay sprawled and exhausted in the aisle of Moribund Advertising's private jet. He feared that no amount of complimentary peanuts would save him now. He was ready to die right then and there, as he was already in heaven. Closing his eyes, he heard clouds and harps and shit.

Then Regan's angel voice called him back, bade him to join her at the window. Weak, groaning, he did as Regan bade. He would have walked through fire for this woman.

"Look," she said, "New York."

Far below them, a brilliant skyline spread out, a cramped constellation of a million lights. It was so beautiful that he almost came again.

But, in the blink of an eye, the beautiful, orgasmy lights were gone. A sudden storm swept over the city, the clouds obscuring the stunning skyline, everything.

From across the aisle, Thorax grunted, "Thank Thor, our journey is near its close, that means you two won't have any clock left for more sex acts in the aisles."

EVISCERATED WITH A PEACH PIT

Nothing about Handjob Krapowitz III's penthouse apartment surprised Margarine Butterfield. Everything in it – the furniture, the Art, the appliances – was expensive and ugly. Just like the man who owned them.

When they first arrived, Mr. Krapowitz declared that they had a few hours to kill before the arrival of Ms. Moribund. Margarine feared that they would spend that time bumping uglies, but her horny boss trundled off, announcing that he was going to have a nice, long soak in the bath. Over his shoulder, he instructed her not to touch anything. After several curse-filled minutes, she figured out how to work the TV and found her favorite film, *Terms of Endearment*, playing on Nearly Classic Movies Television (NCMT). She spent the next few hours with her feet up, drinking scotch from a bottle that she found secreted in a formerly locked cabinet. Once, during a commercial break, she took a dump in a potted plant near the balcony.

During the climactic final scene of the film, where Debra Winger eviscerates Shirley MacLaine with a peach pit, there came a thunderous knock on the front door. It scared Margarine all the way down to her very soul. She sat up, trying to regulate her breathing, waiting for her heart to come back to earth.

"The bitch is early," cried Mr. Krapowitz from the

bathroom. Another knock. If possible, louder. "That fucking lazy doorman, I'll have his job for this!"

"He's already paid the ultimate price," said Margarine in a strange voice, though, to her, it sounded as if someone else was speaking for her. Thinking for her.

"What? What did you just say?" Mr. Krapowitz called.

"Nothing."

"Well, okay then. Just get your clothes off, lay down on the floor, and look like you've been having a good time. I'll be out in a minute."

But Margarine could barely hear her boss. Her ears were filled with beautiful static. Something was pulling her toward the door, like gravity or cinnamon rolls. As if she were ensnared in a dream, she stumbled forward, dropping the bottle of scotch. It may or may not have shattered on the onyx floor.

"Margarine, what the hell was that noise? Are you getting your clothes off and your smile on?"

More knocking. Margarine couldn't tell if it was inside her head or out.

Looking through the peephole, the old lady spied who – or, more precisely what – was on the other side of the door, raring to get in.

"It's not Regan," she said to no one in particular.

"Then... then who the hell is it?" Mr. Krapowitz called out. Even though she was miles away from him, Margarine could hear him tying a robe around himself, see his skinny legs, feel his heart pounding in his pigeon chest.

She smiled; he had a good reason to be scared.

Through her smile, she said, "There's a big bad wolf at your door, Mr. Krapowitz."

"What? Whatever you do, Margarine, do not open that door! I'll call security."

She could hear his hands shaking as he picked up the phone.

Margarine said, "You're too late."

He let the phone drop. "Wait, what... what are you saying out there? I can't hear you."

She opened the door a crack, keeping the chain lock in place. The man outside was so large, she couldn't see all of him. He stuck his giant, sweaty face in the door crack. "Who the hell are you, old lady?"

"I guess you could call me a sex slave. Who are you?"

"They call me Asiago."

"Have you come to cause physical damage to Mr. Krapowitz?"

After a short shrug. "Probably."

As lightning flashed overhead, she slid the chain over.

EMOTIONAL SEAWEED

"Well, this is unexpected," said Regan, lightning flashing overhead.

They stood over the body of the doorman, who, even post-mortem, was doing his job by blocking the entrance of Krapowitz's building. His head had been bashed in, blood was everywhere. Despite the fact that he'd been present at sixty-four murder scenes recently, Moses never got used to death. The metallic smell mostly. They way it crawled up your nasal passages and pried your brain up to see if anyone was home. Death still had the power to turn his stomach, make him look away.

Not Regan, for she was as brave as she was beautiful. She stared down upon the body as if it were an ottoman she was considering buying.

"This be not good," announced Thorax, raising his sword.

Moses wanted to tell him: NO SHIT. But he held his tongue, as he often did around the hot-headed garden gnome.

"Let's look on the bright side, maybe someone has done our job for us," Regan said gaily as she stepped over the body and disappeared into the building. With his short legs, Thorax trod across the body, which seemed to bring him happiness. Following his companions, Moses screwed his eyes shut. Of course, he could still feel the blood crawling up his nose.

Behind him, Moses heard a peel of thunder, followed by a low deep sound that certainly sounded like the growl of a large animal. But that couldn't be; they were in the middle of the city.

Despite the dead doorman and the fact that he was about to help a magical creature snuff out yet another human life, Moses should have been on top of the world. His killing spree was about to end. Whatever happened tonight, the sun would rise in a few hours and Thorax would become a statue again, his mother would return to normal, and Moses would be freed from his indentured servitude.

Not to mention he had Regan and her strap-on and all that fucking.

But Moses didn't feel happy or free. Even though the muzak in the elevator was Moses' favorite song ever, *Sweet Home Alabama*, he couldn't shake the feeling of dread that clung to him like emotional seaweed. He could feel that something was going to happen, something bad. Something worse than just a regular old murder.

CALLING OFF THE WHOLE MURDER THING

"Well, that's unexpected," said Regan as they stepped off the elevator.

The door to Krapowitz's penthouse, where she'd been numerous times whenever Aileen Krapowitz was busy with one of her many rind-related events, was ajar. Coming from inside was the sound of an old woman laughing, cackling actually. The open door and the laughing sent a chill down Regan's spine and for a second she considered turning around, ducking back into the elevator that was playing that horrible Lynyrd Skynyrd song, and calling off the whole murder thing.

But she knew she would never do such a thing. She had to follow through on the killing. She was Regan Moribund, she always finished what she started.

Gritting her teeth, she turned on her companions.

"Come on," she said, hoping to sound more confident than she felt, "let's roll!"

She dashed through the open door.

THERE WAS BLOOD

"Well, that's unexpected," said Regan Moribund as she entered the penthouse apartment with some handsome young thing and an ugly looking midget with a sword. Looking down at the body of Krapowitz, adorned with a matching pair of bullet holes in his chest, Regan's eyes grew to nearly the size of her tits. Although they looked natural, Quentin knew that they were fake. He'd been the one to schedule the appointment. He went with her to the plastic surgeon, held her hand through the whole ordeal, and had told her every day since how real they looked, per her orders.

Gun raised, Asiago stepped forward. "Regan Moribund, we finally meet."

She looked up at the killer, but her gaze quickly shifted to her assistant, who was standing behind the man with the gun. "Quentin, what are you doing here?"

Crocodile tears came fast and furious. "He made me do it, the brute kidnapped me, forced me to have sex with him again and again, and made me lead him here."

Without lowering his weapon, Asiago turned on his lover. "That's crazy talk, Quent, you know that the sex was consensual, and mind-blowing."

Knowing that it was now or never, Quentin picked up a nearby chair, onyx covered with gold filigree, and smashed it over Asiago's head. The late nights at the gym paid off. The chair shattered.

The only problem: Asiago didn't crumple as Quentin imagined. In fact, he looked completely unfazed. Except for the look of horror that twisted his face.

"Quent, baby doll, whatever are you doing?"

The young man's answer came in the form of another chair, which he smashed against the killer's cranium. Again, the brute didn't go down, didn't budge. But a bright shiny tear slid down his cheek.

"Quent, my little love bird, I'm begging you to stop all this foolishness."

Another chair. The same result. Only now Asiago's forehead was cut, there was blood. A trickle.

Covered with sweat from his exertions, Quentin stood there, wishing he'd spent more of his time at the gym pumping iron instead of standing around studying the male form. He was beginning to understand that he might not survive this night.

"Quent, dearest, I can't believe that we're having our first lover's spat in front of all these strangers. It's undignified. Oh my, not another chair, this is getting tiring."

Another chair. The last one. When the sound of it smashing over the thug's head died away and the thug was still standing, Quentin stood there, defeated. Both men were now crying hot tears of rage.

"Die, Doodles, die!" screamed Regan's assistant.

"That tears it. Goodbye, my lovely," said Asiago and he fired once, twice, thrice.

READY TO KILL EVERYONE, EVERYTHING

With tears falling like the blood fell from his forehead injury, Asiago turned away from Quentin's body. Though he was a hired killer, he usually he didn't get angry. Emotion could ruin a hit. But now, with the love of his life dead, Asiago was thoroughly miffed. Ready to kill everyone, everything. Moribund, her boyfriend, the ugly midget, even the old sex slave who'd let them in. Obviously she was nuts, as she was, through all this, standing in the corner, laughing.

Well aware that he only had two bullets left, he decided to take out Regan first, fulfilling his contract. But when he aimed his gun at her nice rack, her boyfriend leapt in front of her, stupid hippie.

His voice shaking, the boyfriend, "Okay, everyone, let's just all take a chill pill and mellow out."

Not a big fan of medication, Asiago pulled the trigger.

While waiting for blood to spill and bone to shatter, a strange thing happened. Moving faster than humanly possible, the midget jumped in front of the hippie, raising his sword. The bullet smacked the blade, ricocheted away.

It struck the batty old woman in the throat. A lot of blood, buckets of the stuff. No longer cackling, she fell to the floor, dead. No one really marked the passing of her life, as they had more pressing matters to deal with.

Asiago knew that he had to make this last shot count. First things first, he had to kill the midget. That fucker was dangerous.

Before he could complete this task, the killer was distracted by the sound of flapping wings and harp music. He turned toward the balcony as a man flew out of the storm and into the apartment. Naked, wings. It was the same dude from Chaps in Chaps. The one he'd killed already, the one who'd exploded into a million little bits.

"Hey assholes," the angel thing said, "cut this killing shit out."

YET ANOTHER BRIEF BURST OF HISTORY

Hello. I'm Bernard. Thanks to the wings and harps and shit, some people think I'm an angel, others think I'm a fairy, whatever floats your boat. My job for the last few millennia has been to keep the peace on planet earth.

Quite rightly, you could point out that I've done a pretty shitty job. Decades of war, terrorist groups, Canadian football. I'll take the heat for those, but you humans have to admit that you're not much fucking help. Someone cuts you off in traffic and you try to run them off the road. Some teacher gives you a bad grade and come back to school armed. Someone calls your deity by a different name and you start pounding your plowshares into swords.

Basically, you fucks aren't worth my time.

So why did I show up to save Regan and Moses? I don't really know. I guess I'm just a sucker for real love, and those two have it in spades. Real love is something that doesn't come down the pike every day.

Besides, Regan has a really nice rack.

Raising my arms, I told the humans to cut their fucking violent shit out. That always shames them enough to get them to stop doing whatever evil they are doing. Then I can turn the assfucks into statues.

But apparently, the armed guy didn't get that memo. The fucker shot me.

WHAT THE FUCK IS THIS NOW

Certainly Asiago, as a former Catholic, feared repercussions for gunning down the angel – which is what this creature had to be, having come back from the dead, plus the ability to fly, not to mention the hot bod – but it had to be done. He'd say some Hail Marys later, after he beat the midget to death.

Imagine Asiago's surprise when he turned to find the unnaturally fast little person already upon him, sword swinging. The unpleasant whistling noise it made while slicing through the air was nothing compared to the gruesome sound it made when slicing through the flesh of his arm. Clean down to the bone. He dropped his bullet-free gun, cried out. Grabbing his wound, he felt hot blood streaming.

Before the little asshole could finish him off, Asiago reared back and kicked the fucker with all of his might. The sword went clitter-clatter on the onyx floor as the midget went sailing. He flew through the air with the greatest of ease and hit an ugly black and white painting of a lemon with a sickening thud. Sliding down the wall, dead as a donut, he left a smear of blood and brain matter.

The hippie, showing more spunk than Asiago liked, rushed forward and tried to retrieve the sword. But even injured, the hitman was quicker. Picking up the sword, he tested its heft. Liking the weapon's feel, he made a mental note to get him one of these bad boys.

He raised said sword to smite the hippie, who, like all hippies, was cowering, waiting for death to come his way.

"Look," said Regan, "you're after me, just let Moses go, please."

Her voice was small. Asiago liked it when his victim's voices dimmed. It meant they'd given up all hope.

The hippie said, "Sweetness, if you're to die, then I want to die by your side."

They hugged. Thinking of his own dead love, Asiago became enraged. Raising the sword, he screamed, "And now you both must die!"

The couple didn't run, didn't fight. They'd lost the will to live. This was the killer's favorite part.

Just as he was about to swing the blade and let it dig deep, he heard a noise behind him.

Turning, he saw a giant pink bear filling the doorway.

"What the fuck is this now?" he asked, just as the bear charged.

FUCK THIS BALONEY

Moses always had a place in his heart for Tenderbear. But not this version. This one had a wild look in his plastic eyes, his fur was matted with blood, and his sailor cap. was AWOL. He looked more like a killing machine than a friendly bear who wanted to help keep your ass clean.

The fascist who was killing everybody didn't even have time to put up a fight when Tenderbear rushed him and ripped his head clean off.

Before the decapitated body crumpled to the floor, the crazed creature turned on Moses and Regan, bearing his teeth.

Moses didn't remember Tenderbear having teeth. Especially ones this sharp.

Reminding himself that this wasn't actually an animal, that there was a man somewhere beneath all that pink carpeting, Moses rushed toward Tenderbear, holding his hands up, begging the man in the bear suit to stop.

One mighty blow from a pink paw sent Moses reeling. He landed on his ass at Regan's feet. Looking up, he saw the woman he loved crying, her face frozen in fear.

That got him back on his feet, ready to battle. Never before had Moses been in a fight, not even in the schoolyard. He could only imitate what he'd seen others do in similar situations. Putting up his dukes, he circled the beast. Tenderbear did the same.

This went on for several seconds, and Moses would have been perfectly content if this dance had gone on forever, but the bear attacked. Grabbing Moses around his quivering midsection and squeezing.

Attempting to keep his shrieking to a minimum, Moses elbowed the bear and slipped out of his grasp, ending up behind him. Remembering a move that had been used against him at an anti-war rally, he locked his arm around Tenderbear's throat and pulled for all he was worth.

A gurgling roar started in Tenderbear's soul and worked its way north. Trying to shake the human loose, the bear stumbled backwards as fast as he could. Moses was crushed against the wall and all the air in his lungs took a vacation. He lost his grip, fell to the floor.

Tenderbear picked him up as if he were a lump of nothing and chomped down on his shoulder. Moses heard bones crunching, felt blood flowing freely outside of his body. He knew the end was nigh.

The bear hurled him across the room, Moses hit the opposite wall hard, crumpled. From his vantage point on the floor. Moses watched Tenderbear, acting like a professional wrestler, flex his muscles and roar loud enough to shake everything loose in Moses' body.

"Get up, Moses," Regan cried. "Get up and fight!"

Moses was about to tell her to mind her own damned business when the angel, who wasn't as dead as everyone suspected, sat up and picked the bullet from his chest, and added, "Yeah, you can do it."

Suddenly filled with confidence in his abilities, Moses leapt to his feet just as Tenderbear was closing in for the kill.

Balling his fist, he lashed out with every fiber in his being. His punch met the advancing bear square in the jaw and knocked his head right off. It landed near the body of the old woman.

For a moment, everyone and everything - time and shit - stood perfectly still.

Moses fully expected to be face-to-face with the dude inside the bear costume. But that wasn't the case. There was no head, no face, nothing. Getting up on his tiptoes, Moses looked down into the suit.

"Jesus' balls," he whispered, "there's no one in here."

"That's impossible," said Regan.

"Nothing's impossible," said the angel. He now seemed much better. He was standing and eating a large sandwich which had magically appeared in his hand.

Thinking of how good that sandwich looked, Moses was distracted when Tenderbear, headless, punched him in the gut.

Clutching his midsection, Moses stumbled backwards and fell against a stupid statue of a golden swan.

His eyes a little dizzy, he spat out a measuring cup's worth of blood and watched a blurry Tenderbear advance upon him. Holding out his paws before him, the sightless animal was not as fast, not as sure, as he had been.

"He can't see," cried Regan. "Use that to your advantage, dumpling!"

"This baloney is fucking awesome," added the angel. He had recovered to the point where he was now hovering above the floor, doing a few simple aerial acrobatics.

As quietly as he could, Moses rolled away from the approaching bear, leaving a trail of blood. The animal didn't even change direction, pawing at the air where his prey had been.

Moses would have liked to roll all the way back to Iowa, but his forward motion was stopped when he encountered something solid. The fascist's headless body.

He wanted to scream, but didn't dare, as that would have given away his position. He knew that later, after all of this mess was over, he would never stop screaming. If he survived.

There was something pressing into the small of Moses' back. Praying it was not the large man's post-mortem erection, he leapt to his feet.

It was Evil Tine, the Sword of Might and Forbearance gleaming with blood.

"I want to fuck this baloney just as much as you want to kill that bear," the angel or whatever he was said.

In one swift move, Moses rose, grasping the sword. Although Awful Tine, the Sword of Might and Forbearance had been in his home for almost a month, he'd never had any interest in it. Not once had Moses asked Thorax about its origins, he'd never so much as touched it. Even hated looking at it as the sword was such a bummer. But in his hands, the sword sang.

With a roar that out-beared Tenderbear, the young

man rushed forward, didn't hesitate as he drove the sword deep into the bear's pink back. The faceless creature couldn't scream, but his pain was evident. He writhed, reaching for the weapon, which was unreachable. Dancing in agony, the bear spun a few times before collapsing. Stopped moving.

With a sigh, Moses, bloodied and battered, joined him on the floor. Closing his eyes, he breathed his last.

ALL'S DEAD THAT ENDS DEAD

"Well," sighed the winged creature, "all's dead that ends dead."

Tears burning, Regan screamed. Staggering through the minefield of dead bodies, she ran to her true love. Kneeling beside Moses, she pulled his corpse to her breast. Her tears mixing with his blood.

"It appears," sighed the winged creature, "that my work here is done."

He flew toward the balcony but Regan screamed, "Stop, please, stop! You're magical, are you not?"

"I can fly, make sandwiches appear out of thin air, you can't kill me, what do you think?"

"Okay, then bring my true love back to me."

The winged creature studied the dead man and his mate. Behind him, streaks of lightning filled the night sky. "Okay, I'll do it because I like you two. But for all the pain Moses Guttchenridder's caused, he will have to pay a price."

"What's that?"

"He will no longer be a handsome hippie. In fact, he will be hideous."

Without hesitation, Regan agreed to this bargain.

Shrugging, the winged creature waved his hand in Moses' general direction and, without waiting to see the effect, flew off into the night, dropping a deuce on the way out.

Regan didn't watch him leave; she only had eyes for her beloved. She waited for what seemed like hours, crying herself dry.

Finally, a shadow passed over Moses' dead face and he began to change. His skin grayed, sagged. His teeth grew and protruded. His hair became unruly, his nose bulbous. All across his face, warts bloomed like tiny volcanoes.

One of his eyes flickered open, a nervous butterfly. His iris was the color of wet cement that would never set. He opened the other eye, that one was the color of dough that would never rise.

His voice nasally, Moses said, "Man, I feel weird."

"All will be well," Regan promised, stroking his oily hair. "All will be well."

THE END OF THE END

Regan was understandably nervous, being on the set of Moses' first television commercial for Krap-Wad toilet paper. All the Krapowitz clan, fresh from Handjob's funeral, was present. Frowning, arms crossed. Glowering.

In the dark shadows of the studio stood Helen Guttchenridder, Moses' mother. She was still in shock over her reanimation and the hideous condition of her son. Her face constantly red from tears. She could barely manage a smile for Regan.

The new head of Moribund Advertising had more to worry about than her future mother-in-law. Just this morning the police had found two dead hookers in the timeshare in Passaic, their butts up in the air, starved to death.

Not to mention this commercial. Her whole career was riding on it.

Regan headed for Moses' dressing room. She tried to come up with some words of encouragement but could think of nothing that she hadn't already said.

When she reached the dressing room door, it flew open and Moses stepped out. He looked so handsome, so majestic, that Regan nearly fainted.

The new Tenderbear costume had been completely redesigned. It was more form-fitting than the old one, with bulging muscles made from foam. Tenderbear's new color was a pleasing, child psychologist-approved, periwinkle. Gone was the sailor cap., replaced by a pith helmet which focus groups found manly, reassuring.

A real smile spread across Regan's face. "You look great, Moses. Are you ready?"

Nodding, he growled his assent.

Grabbing his hand, she led him toward the set – a jungle fashioned entirely out of rolls of toilet paper.

Her smile faltered when she realized that Moses had never growled before in the Tenderbear costume, even when they were alone, having rough sex.

Growling again, Tenderbear squeezed her hand tighter and tighter. *Until the bones in her hand snapped.*

FINIS

A Short But Exciting History of Thicke & Vaney Books
Purveyor of *Fine* to Middling Works

In 1888, Richard Thicke, amateur stevedore and pugilist and Thomas "Vaney" Vanesworthy III, wordsmith and bon vivant, joined forces to start a publishing company, Thicke & Vaney Books. Their goal was to print the finest literary works in all the land. They failed miserably. But over the last century and a half, Thicke & Vaney Books have published many a ripping yarn. In 2016, Thicke and Vaney moved themselves and their business to Saint Paul, Minnesota to escape the nasty weather in London. They failed miserably.

Bix Skahill, professional author, has written several novels. Well, a few. For instance, *Babes in Gangland* and *Dope Tits*. For years he worked for the beast known as Hollywood before being chased out of town in the middle of the night. Mr. Skahill is known as the third most popular writer from Red Oak, Iowa.

www.ingramcontent.com/pod-product-compliance
Lightning Source LLC
Chambersburg PA
CBHW020618120726
47905CB00003B/845